PASSIONATE ORPHAN

PASSIONATE ORPHAN

JOHN B. THOMPSON

CUTTING EDGE

ISBN-13: 978-1-970848-19-9

Published by
Cutting Edge Books
PO Box 8212
Calabasas, CA 91372
www.cuttingedgebooks.com

TABLE OF CONTENTS

Page

CHAPTER ONE—CYRI BECOMES AN ORPHAN 1

CHAPTER TWO—THE OLD BARREL HOUSE 15

CHAPTER THREE—ACY 37

CHAPTER FOUR—HIGH SOCIETY 51

CHAPTER FIVE—THE PRINCESS 59

CHAPTER SIX—CYRI STEPS OUT 79

CHAPTER SEVEN—AN AFFAIR ENDED 108

CHAPTER EIGHT—ABSALOM O'MARA 121

CHAPTER NINE—A NURSE IN LOVE 143

CHAPTER TEN—LESTER BIDS GOODBYE 167

CHAPTER ELEVEN—AN ORPHAN TAKES HER MAN 178

CHAPTER ONE
—CYRI BECOMES AN ORPHAN

I T HAPPENED a long time ago, but even then people didn't talk about it much. Fine families who have wealth are in a manner elevated from the mass of people, and are accorded tacit privileges and a certain tolerance which people wouldn't allow one of their own number.

So when it was talked around that old Dagger Macambre had beaten Merle Malnoir to within an inch of his life there was little if any resentment. Merle was not a community paragon, but neither, on the other hand, was Dagger Macambre who was reputed to have drunk half a gallon of whiskey a day for thirty years.

Alphonse Quebedeaux was an old man then and had been there at the time. Such news as filtered out had come from him.

He had gone to the Macambre plantation to make a horse trade because Dagger not only owned the best horses in the country but held a reputation for close trading that Alphonse resented. He thought he deserved the title himself.

He will tell the story today if pressed and lubricated with a sufficiency of bourbon whiskey.

Merle had been working at the Macambre plantation for several months and had grown very fond of Dagger's beautiful daughter, Marlene, a situation which Dagger found vastly humorous at first, then vastly disconcerting. When Dagger was disconcerted he habitually vented his spleen upon the hapless victim, using a twisted hickory walking stick which bore many a stain attesting to the violence of his temper.

Dagger, however, was not in his own estimation an unfair man, and the sight of Marlene and Merle clenched in the chimney corner had made him furious because he hadn't known the depth of their feeling. Instead of flying into a storming rage he turned on his heels and disappeared around the corner of the old river house. He went to the front verandah where he sat until he spied Merle on the way to the stables and followed him.

"Seen you awhile ago," said Dagger, beating the heel of his boot with the hickory walking stick. He had small respect for the niceties of speech.

Merle turned his head and flushed red. "Yes, sir."

"Thatair all you got to say?"

Merle gulped and began to lose some of his ruddy cast.

"Mean to stand there and tell me you think Marlene might be fer the likes of you? Goddamned plantation tramp, hoss polisher … humpf! Lemme see another sich act and out you go … if you can walk." He turned and stalked away, old but straight and powerfully built. His hair was still raven black and his hawk-like nose was as thin as a blade, given to sniffing sarcastically at times.

He stalked back to the house and cornered Marlene in the living room. "Seen that little cuddly scene back of the chimney awhile ago."

Marlene, who was afraid of her father, sank back in her chair. She was a slender girl with enough curves to make her attractive. Her face was spare but well boned and her eyes were deeply, mysteriously blue. Her lips were passionately curved, damp and red without the new fangled paint which her father refused to let her use.

"Well, cat got your tongue?"

"No, sir."

"Then what you got to say?"

"Nothing, sir."

"Humpf ... thought not. Lemme catch you again and I'll tan the hide off you ... in fact...." He pulled her out of the chair to a standing position. "Bend down!"

There was fear in her gasp that did not seem engendered by the simple request.

She obeyed, trembling. Dagger's face was hard and expressionless as he watched her.

"Is this all right, sir?"

"Bend lower. I got something for you. Next time you'll remember."

"Please, father ..." Her great eyes filled and overflowed. "Please don't do that to me."

"None of your sniveling," he rasped, his breath coming faster.

Slowly she bent lower ... with great reluctance, looking like a delectable mermaid emerging from the waves, pink and white and utterly lovely. He approached her, his hands clutching ... opening and closing, his eyes flaming over her virginal beauty, his tongue licking out like the head of a snake.

His hands sank into the flesh of her shoulder making her cry out, then with a gentleness that was not in keeping with his subsequent action he laid her across his lap, heedless of her sobs, and stared at the melodic curve of her hips and buttocks. He caressed their swells avidly, then seemed to remember why he had made her assume the position. His face changed and was blackened with a scowl, his lips raised in a snarl and he withdrew the hand as though it had been resting on a hot stove. With hard skin-reddening blows he spanked her until her fundament was crimson and her cries resounded through the house.

Five minutes later he was holding her sobbing body closely in his arms, tears streaking his own face. "You're all I have left of *her*," he muttered, "and before any other man'll get you, I'll kill you."

It had happened several times before they were caught; even though Merle was afraid of the old man, he was young, and Marlene was hardly seventeen and starved for affection. That same day, after spanking her, Dagger had mounted his horse and galloped away, telling the stable boy that he was going to River Oaks and wouldn't be back until dark.

Merle, who had hidden and heard, leaped out of the loft and sped toward the house, running with the easy grace of youth.

In his arms Marlene cried again ... hard and bitterly, but she recovered quickly. Her father's beating and curious actions had had a peculiar effect on her, making Merle's arms seem a haven where she wanted to hide, to confide all her hopes and fears ... and to undress again.

The actions of her body were slight, but Merle was experienced and noticed them quickly, being even quicker to take advantage. They were in the parlor but she was led to the bedroom where Merle plied his experience to good effect. His lips were hot on hers, and her body seemed broken by the pressure of his arms, but she only whined a little and let his efforts be rewarded. Again her body flexed, although she scarcely knew it until, horrified, she looked with lust for the first time at the body of a man. Her own feeling seemed at the moment less than his, but even the horror she felt could not stem the awful surge of reaction that inundated her. Her arms were weak and the touch of him, from toes to mouth, was of such swooning ecstasy that she made no effort to thwart him. He laid her upon the bed and kissed the hollow between her breasts, the little creases made by the junction of arm and shoulder, her neck and finally her ears, sending her body into a frenzy of reaction.

"Merle … don't … please don't …" He couldn't have escaped had he tried, because her arms were cords of rope across his back, and, slender but strong, they embraced him with terrible insistence. Still begging him not to, but with her body demanding its due, her pleas soon turned to deep-throated echoes of the first song ever sung by woman.

There were other times when Dagger was away, but one time he came back unexpectedly. He was riding toward Twin Oaks when he met Alphonse Quebedeaux.

"Comme ca va m'sieur Macambre," said Alphonse reining up. He was riding a white maned Palomino that took Dagger's eyes instantly.

"Bien …" Dagger's greeting was short as it always was when he saw a horse he liked.

"You like the horse?" asked the former.

Dagger nodded casually. "Pretty good. Legs too small, though."

Quebedeaux grinned. It had begun and would go on like this for a long time.

"That Rex horse," said Alphonse as they rode toward the barn after an hour's haggling, "is too old."

"Too old …" Dagger bristled. "Bet you he's not over a year older than your horse … and look at the blood lines."

"Look at the horse," argued Alphonse as they rode into the barn and dismounted.

Their feet had hardly touched the dirt floor when a despairing cry came to their ears through the open door of the cotton seed room that was not twenty feet from them.

"Oh, God, Merle … Merle … Oh, closer, closer, Merle … *Merle."*

Dagger's head went up like a winding pointer and he headed straight for the cotton seed room and into the open door, leaving

Alphonse trembling with trepidation and excitement which he could sense but not name.

Merle tumbled head first from the room, his head split open and bleeding. He leaped to his feet and tried to flee, but the old man was too fast for him. He had hardly taken the first step when the heavy stick cracked solidly against his head again and he went down. Cursing, his face almost bursting with furious blood, Dagger stood over him and beat him with hard swinging blows of the stick until his body was covered with blood blisters, welts and horrible ragged lacerations that seeped dark blood slowly. Marlene leaped at her father and tried to tear the stick from his grasp, but she was powerless, and for her interference she received a crushing blow in the mouth from his fist that knocked her reeling against Alphonse who caught and held her, hardly knowing what to do. Finally he let her gently to the floor of the barn, and stepping in close, caught and wrested the stick from Dagger, stepped back and prepared for the worst. To his surprise Dagger leaned wearily back against the barn wall and passed his hand slowly over his face, streaking the spattered blood.

For a long time he stayed motionless then heaved up heavily. "Take the Rex horse ..."

"Even trade?" asked Alphonse eagerly.

"No ... take him. No trade. I give him to you. Please ... don't tell anyone ..."

Alphonse felt a knot tighten in his throat. "I don't want a horse for being a little decent."

"*Take the horse.* Go, and don't come back anymore." Alphonse took the horse and left, a picture engraved in his mind of the horribly beaten man stretched in the dirt of the barn floor, the seductive girl, slim, graceful and lovely, crumpled near him, unconscious and bleeding from her battered lips. It was a picture he'd take to his grave.

A week later it was all over. Dagger had died two nights after the incident, and the girl was found to be pregnant. Merle didn't die, but for weeks it was thought he would, and when he finally could totter around on his own legs he was no match for the begging girl who, having no one to turn to, turned to the man most responsible for her plight.

When the creditors were paid and the bank satisfied, she barely had the clothes on her back. And Merle's little shack at least had a good tin roof.

To this day it is unknown exactly what name the child was intended to bear because at the christening the mother was reeling drunk and supported by a neighbor who, from her look of tight lipped disapproval, would have preferred to let her fall.

Father Francioni, the priest, accepted the situation with Jesuitical fortitude if not approval, carrying on in the face of distractions that might well have balked a lesser man, and when Cyritta Malnoir became the girl's name, it was the nearest he could come to spelling the noise which at the moment of question had burbled from Marlene's mouth.

That night as he prepared for bed Father Francioni was still not certain whether he had blessed a name or a curse.

Cyri soon learned that, for her, life held little that was not centered about a strong back and hard work. She learned a great deal because Father Francioni gave her work to do, fed her well and taught her assiduously, for which he was rewarded with a mind which at times astounded and not infrequently dismayed him.

Although she worked hard and frequently, because she wanted to eat, and though there was always liquor in her home, there was rarely food of the sort all active children need. She liked best to work for the priest because his jobs were simple, easy and there were always the lessons which she loved. Better still, she loved their talks during which she would ask question after question, some of which made the good father sweat.

Cyri's mother died one night, trying to ascertain whether it was true, as her husband maintained, that whiskey did not grow on trees. After consuming a quart of gin acquired in a manner which needs no exploring here, she fell head first from the one starved tree of which their yard boasted. It wasn't much of a tree what with the ground around it packed as hard as concrete, ax wounds in its scabrous bark, hen nests nailed to its trunk, and the strangling embrace of a clothes-line made of barbed wire, but it was tall enough to break the woman's neck. As the mother had been drunk at the christening, so also was Merle, the husband, drunk at the funeral, steadied by the ham-sized hand of Alton Quebedeau, Alphonse's stalwart son.

Cyri was there, her face composed and beautiful, and throughout the service it did not so much as quiver. On the way home Alphonse, now bent and showing the ravages of age, was moved to grief for the girl, and said as much.

His wife snorted. "Not a single tear …" The buggy dropped a wheel in a hole and jolted them severely. Alphonse slapped the aging horse gently on the hips with the reins as his wife continued. "Not a tear did she shed. Not one cry, not even blinking the eyes."

"People who cry," retorted her husband witheringly, "are sorry. Why should she be sorry?"

The answer to his question was such that his wife deemed it politic to remain silent and she suffered the old man to let the buggy wheel dip into another pothole without protest.

When Cyri decided to explore the warmth of the barn one afternoon with a certain lad of her acquaintance, T'Cal, morals were in no way concerned simply because she knew nothing of them. Father Francioni had explained to her the crucifixion and the resurrection, the miracles and the benevolence of the Most Holy Mother, but his curriculum steered a wide course around morals. This was true only in the case of Cyri, because the father could smite sin hip and thigh to a congregation who expected it, but privately he held curious convictions about morals which might account for his being priest in a small starveling parish. He had once told Alphonse Quebedeaux, whom it was impossible to shock or surprise, that morals continued their merry way despite all ecclesiastical exhorting, and he often wondered to how many of his flock his exhortations had conjured up a particular bit of sinning, to be done as soon as it was feasible and safe. Alphonse had grinned toothlessly and wisely and said nothing. Cyri knew right from wrong after a fashion, but even this had never been visited hard upon her because she was healthy of body and mind, needing none of the usual bizarre outlets for a twisted psyche. She took what was hers with authority, and rendered unto others what was theirs with the same freedom.

She had put out a large washing that day, eaten an early supper and was seated on the back porch of T'Cal's mother's house, talking to T'Cal.

"It's raining," he said to her as they sat on the back porch.

She nodded. "Yes, it is."

"I'll bet the barn is all nice and warm. There's one room all full of cotton."

"I'll bet so too."

"You want to go? We could dig holes in the cotton and get good and warm."

"If you're cold, why don't you go in the kitchen?"

"I ain't that cold. I just thought it would be fun to go in the barn."

"O.K. Let's go."

T'Cal let her climb through the window ahead of him, saying this entrance would make it secret and mysterious, sort of. He hung back and felt a hot flush as she exposed her slim strong legs, the melodic curve of her under-developed but promising hips. Quickly he reached out his hand and touched her, bracing himself for the inevitable slap, but she only giggled and tumbled headlong into the soft new cotton. His head reeling with new confidence and the promise his touch had offered, he climbed in after her. Beside her on the cotton, his nerve failed again and he resorted to talk. "Nice, ain't it?"

"Unh hunh."

"Warm, ain't it?"

"Unh hunh."

"Did that make you mad?"

"What?"

"What I just did."

"No … it sort of tickled … funny like."

"Did it tickle good?"

"Kind of."

He pulled himself close to her and the trembling hand became active again. She wriggled a little as his hot moist hand touched her. He stopped, his ragged breath showing the state of his nerves. "That tickle?"

"A little."

Emboldened, he essayed greater liberties, enjoying a sense of victory as a rigor ran over her. Something else had happened too. Her body grew strangely restless and seemed to move of its own volition. Her face turned toward him and the look in her eyes made his heart throb heavily. Her breath was coming faster and he couldn't bear to look at her face because he felt mean and bad. He looked again, however, and this time he couldn't help himself … he kissed her on the lips. She responded in a manner that surprised them both. It was nothing like the kisses he had stolen in his fifteen years of life. He noticed that her thighs had been taut and resisting, but were not flaccid. Sweat broke out on his forehead and he removed the hand to tug at her dress where it buttoned at the throat. The shock of her erect young breasts tensed his mouth, and he noticed another rigor and a spasmodic clutch of her arms about his neck. Then he realized that things were ripe for whatever he desired to do.

The weight of his body forced a querulous little sound from her throat, then a gasp of pain.

"That hurt?"

"Not much," she admitted. "It …" She shut her eyes and clutched him convulsively.

Later, as he lay on his back letting the results play with his muscles, she sat up and inspected him with interest. "You're made like Pappa."

"Sure," he said casually. "All men are built like that."

"Must be handy … in a way," she said.

"It is. Does it hurt any more?"

"No. It just hurt once … a little … T'Cal?"

"What?"

"That was nice."

"Sure … again?"

"Unh hunh. Will you kiss me again … and you know … and sort of …" She moved toward him while he watched hungrily. He didn't speak, but proved to her that he could do everything just as he had before.

There were other rainy afternoons when the work was done and afternoons that were not rainy. Then came the afternoon when there was, in addition to T'Cal, Shem Latigue. Shem was older and a lot more sophisticated, therefore he demanded priority, but Cyri would have none of it.

"T'Cal first," she said.

After T'Cal came Shem with a great deal more finesse and experience, but for some reason she did not like him, and afterward she told T'Cal.

"Don't ever tell anyone else about us. I don't like Shem."

"But he's a friend of mine," he protested.

"Must I let all your friends? Aren't you proud that I want just you?"

T'Cal, being no intellectual, was easily flattered. He kissed her and allowed his hand to roam objectively because he knew she liked it. "Sure, Cyri ... just me and you."

A belated flicker of intelligence revealed to T'Cal that if too many knew about Cyri someone might ease him out, and this he did not want. He thought of Shem's loud bragging mouth and shuddered.

Cyri, after the news had been properly broadcast, shuddered also, because every boy she knew desired to entice her to some sheltered place. This she neither wanted, nor appreciated, and in a burst of rage at T'Cal after she had come to realize what had happened, struck him a fearful blow in the face and never returned to his mother's house to work.

Father Francioni heard about it and pondered upon what he should or could do, there being a wide variance between the two. He could send her to a convent, but Father Francioni held certain personal opinions of convents which would have caused him to suffer had he made them public. The things he could do were few and required more money than he ever had at any one time. Father Francioni was a very poor politician, a somewhat sarcastic man with a devastating penetration that did not reap friends in clerical circles ... therefore, he was a poor man, as are all politicians who strive to be honest.

Alphonse Quebedeaux had all of the padre's keenness of penetration, the same flair for unguarded sarcasm, without suffering from it. It was he, therefore, who stepped into the breach when a hue and cry arose, demanding that the girl be ridden out on a rail liberally tarred and feathered. This last was a suggestion of the Anglo-Saxon element long noted for the rigidity of their visible morals. That this rigidity is not necessarily subscribed to after dark is a matter for psychologists to explain.

Coincident with the hue and cry was an occurrence at home which did not trouble Cyri's morals a great deal, since it has been shown that she was neither moral nor immoral, having an imperfect knowledge of either in a social sense. Her father came home drunk one night, and upon seeing her stride through the room clad in nothing, became suddenly aware that in his house he had reared a woman of singular beauty. His wife had been dead four months, and not having the money to buy anything but liquor and having none of his early dark dashing looks, Malnoir was suffering. It is not known whether Merle suffered from the pangs of conscience, but it is known that he got in to bed with his daughter. It can be guessed what his intentions were and possibly he can be forgiven for not knowing what he was getting into, but a surprise awaited him which was to be his last surprise in life.

Cyri probably did not think of the morals involved when she felt her father's arms about her and his whiskeyed breath in her face, but it is certain that she did not mistake his intentions … and she resented them, because she did not like him and for no other reason.

Merle drew her close, becoming more excited than he could ever remember, feeling with drunken delight the long velvety textured body of his daughter and the pricking touch of her firm, youthful breasts.

Of a sudden he felt a pain in his throat and he couldn't breathe any more. The body that had been all softness, beauty, and desire, suddenly was transformed into an animal-like thing of steel and whalebone from which his whiskey-weakened, mal-nurtured muscles could not escape. He strove to cry out, to make any sort of noise, to escape from the steel taloned thing on his breast that was crushing the life from him. Fancifully striped geometric figures whirled madly through his sodden brain, momentarily clear for the first time·in months. Very clearly he saw that he could not escape her. His beating hands were as futile as the wings of an imprisoned moth. A world full of pure sweet air was shut off from his tortured lungs for all time by a pair of slim brown hands whose grace and nimbleness at work belied their crushing strength. His brain grew confused again, and the weakness of his limbs became a refuge into which he slipped, feeling a strange and inexplicable comfort.

CHAPTER TWO
—THE OLD BARREL HOUSE

S HERIFF Delieux sat in his armchair and studied the chess board before him. Let his jailer and deputies play bouray and scream themselves hoarse with Gallic excitement, he preferred his chess, although there was but one man in town who could play with him. Alphonse Quebedeaux sat back on the other side and cackled gleefully. "Now do somethings. That all I got to say … do somethings."

The sheriff shook his head slowly. "I ain't the best tonight. I guess I need sleeping."

"You need thinking," said Alphonse, brutally exposing his gums in a grin. "That's what you need."

The sheriff nodded heavily. "Tomorrow, she's another day and we'll see what is needing who."

A deputy poked his head in the door. "Dat gal of Merle's here. She want to see you."

"O.K.," he said, eager for anything to cut short Alphonse's inevitable crowing when he won a game of chess.

Cyri walked into the room nodding respectfully. "Good evening, Mr. Delieux … Mr. Quebedeaux … I've just killed my father."

There was a short stiff silence during which time the sheriff's brain reacted a lot faster than it had the hour previously. "Unh hunh ... so you say. Why did you kill him?" He did not doubt her word, she had been too bluntly frank about it.

"He tried to ..." She stopped short, not because she was embarrassed, but because she didn't know what to call it. To ... well, he got in bed with me and ..."

The sheriff raised a hasty hand and felt his face grow crimson, but she told him anyway in flat, pointed language what her father had tried to do.

"Guess we'd better take a look," said the sheriff to Alphonse, who had risen and put on his black hat, grinning like a gargoyle. He could feel the sheriff's embarrassment if he could not share it. Alphonse was too old and had seen too much to be embarrassed by things that did not concern him.

"Sure, I go with you."

"You stay here with the deputies till I get back," Delieux told the girl.

"Oy, no, no, no," burst out old Alphonse. "We take her along too ... mebby she prefair to come."

"Yes, sir. I'd rather come."

"How come?" asked the sheriff in French to Alphonse.

"Because I don't trust your deputies any more than I do half the boys in town who have heard about the girl and have tried to take her into the woods or the barn."

"That's correct, sir," she told them in the same language and this time Alphonse's face grew as red as had the sheriff's. They had both assumed that she didn't speak French for the same reason that many Frenchmen make the mistake ... she didn't look French. Her association with the many French children (River Oaks is two-thirds French) had given her fluent command of the language.

"W'at you gon' to do?" asked Alphonse two hours later as they drank strong black coffee at the jail.

"I ought to put her in the jails," said Delieux refusing to look at the old man.

Alphonse squeaked angrily. "You just like all the peoples here in town, you ... a fool. W'at she should do, let him sleep with her? Then it get out and you put them both in jail?"

Delieux squirmed. "What would you do if you was sheriff?"

Alphonse leaned over and whispered in his ear and the sheriff brightened. "Sure, that's good idea."

Dawn found Cyri standing out on the Airline Highway, looking uncertainly at the passing cars. She was frightened, but what old Alphonse had told her was even more frightening and she did not pretend to understand.

He had put five dollars in her hand. "Now you are making escapes," he told her. "You go at New Orleans and get you a jobs and nobody will ever fine you."

She had thanked him and walked away from the jail house. She had on her best clothes, a white cotton blouse and a cheap serge skirt that was too short, dingy, faded and patched in three places. On her feet were a pair of sneakers that had belonged to her mother. She would have preferred to be barefooted, but she knew that the road would be hard on her feet and she had not the faintest notion of how far New Orleans was from River Oaks and it never occurred to her that someone might pick her up.

The first was a man who should have been old enough to know better, but it took only three minutes, part of which was taken up parking on a lonely sugar cane road, to teach him. Once the car was stopped, he became amorous which might not have been repugnant were it not for the fact that the man was probably sixty-five years old, needed a bath, and had a terrible breath. One sound, well-delivered blow from a rock hard fist and a spray of colorful lights exploded in his brain. It was several active seconds before he could open the door and fall out to escape the clawing, tearing animal whom he had picked for an easy thing.

Back on the road, Cyri was picked up by a youngster who also parked, but he was nice, personable, smelled good, and he didn't try to manhandle her. In fact, so suave was his approach, that Cyri was aiding him avidly before the boy hardly realized that he had found someone who felt much as he himself did regarding certain matters; so, they spent two delightful hours screened from the rushing cars by a growth of heavy weeds. Cyri sank back on the cushions, unashamed, relaxed and filled to repletion with chocolate candy the boy had bought for another girl but, deciding that the other girl would probably deserve it less than Cyri, had opened it and shared it with her.

She reached over and touched him, exploratorily. He jumped and said, "Don't do that!"

"Why?" she wanted to know. "That's the way you did me."

"Well ... I'm a boy ..."

"Well ... I'm a girl."

The lad squirmed. "Sure, but ... anyhow don't ..." A gasp stopped him and though she had produced in him heights of performance to which he had never risen before, she enticed him even further till at last they lay almost comatose from weariness and satiation.

It was almost night when Beverly Babcock picked her up. The sight of the man repelled her in some strange way, but he did not offer to harm her. He was effeminate, with an unmanly voice, smelled heavenly from some expensive perfume, and, though dressed in masculine clothing, he managed to give them the appearance of femininity.

He took her to an expensive hotel where they registered as father and daughter, and the next morning took her to a very exclusive shop and bought her a complete wardrobe, even to tennis shorts and T-shirts.

That night, under the influence of a strange minty-smelling drink, she had fallen in love with the filmy underthings he had bought her, although she did not the brassiere and only wore it because it was pretty. She had bathed lengthily and luxuriously in a tub brimming with hot water into which she had ladled half a pint of Beverly's expensive bath salts. She had put on a crimson silk robe, sat in front of the mirror brushing her soft, smoky, black hair till it glistened in the light falling below her shoulders.

Beverly swigged the last of his minty drink and looked at her face reflected in the mirror. It was placidly beautiful, without a sign of worry or conflict. Her great eyes were the most delightful green and the smooth curve of her cheek and the proud set of her thin patrician nose made his mouth water. Her lips were full and sensual, imbued with their own natural redness, a striking contrast to the rich Jersey cream tan of her skin.

He walked over to her. "Enjoying yourself, Cyri?"

"Oh, yes ... thank you. You've been very nice."

"Like your clothes?"

"Yes, sir ... I love them."

"Take them off." His squeaky voice was harsh.

"Take ... take them off?"

"Of course ... take them off. You can't sleep in them."

"But you bought me a gown to sleep in."

Beverly bit his lips with vexation and walked to the little dresser where he mixed another drink from the large bottle and ginger ale. He quaffed half of it and turned around.

She stood uncertainly, wondering why he wanted her to undress, striking such an unbelievably lovely picture that Beverly's heart leaped with sudden pain. She stood in mid-stride, her small waist and swelling hips encased in a glassy sheath of white nylon and to her breasts clung a net of sheer, almost non-sensical, support.

Something deep within her spoke it's soundless voice and her body responded while she stood in her questioning attitude. Slim, lushly curved, her face a study in innocence, her visible reaction combined to drive Beverly a little mad.

With a cry, he lunged forward and fell at her feet, his arms embracing her. For a second she was frightened, then more amazed than ever. His next act she was totally unprepared for, and it sent a flash of white hot emotion, sensation, and utter surprise through her. A sharp gasping sound came from her lips and had he not held her erect, she would have fallen. Never in all her short, but eventful life had anything weakened her so overpoweringly. He picked her up and carried her to the bed where he lost all semblance of control, ceasing an hour later, with the girl a mass of nerves that were like white hot wires crawling within her, but so weak from the ordeal that she could scarcely move. He was a kind and generous man who had befriended her, but had he asked her to repeat this performance she could not have done it.

The thought sent a wave of revulsion through her which was immediately dispelled by a throb that set her gradually relaxing muscles to quivering again. It had been a shattering experience, she could not deny that for all its post-climactic revulsion. While he bathed, she fell into a dreamless sleep and when she woke the next morning, he was gone.

She bathed and relived the night's experience with mingled emotions. Cyri was just seventeen, but she had experienced more than many women twice her age and had ascended the heights of the fiercest passions, heights which few women have the capacity to reach. Of all these things she was conscious in a sense, but at the same time she did not treat them as unusual or out of the ordinary. She had the simple person's faith in the future, refusing to worry about the present. Another, upon waking and finding herself deserted would have flown into a fright … or a rage, but not Cyri. When she returned from her bath, Beverly had come back bringing with him a man in a very smart uniform, rolling a breakfast cart.

"Ready to eat, my dear?" he asked in an unctious voice for the benefit of the bell hop.

She smiled and nodded. "Oh, yes … I'm starved." She sat and in so doing revealed a considerable length of smooth tanned leg which almost made the man drop the coffee pot.

When he had gone, Beverly addressed her severely. "Never bare yourself to another man like that."

"But last night you took all the clothes off me."

He had the grace to flush. "Quite … quite, but I'm different."

"In what way," she wanted to know and her calm green eyes made him feel nailed to the wall, consequently he floundered and she noticed it.

"You are too young to know about those things," he countered lamely. "Just don't do it again."

"Not even to you?"

Beverly brushed a deposit of sweat from his brow. "That's different. As I said, don't let other men see your body. With me it's all right."

"Yes," she said calmly, her eyes becoming harder than ever to bear, "you told me that you didn't give me a reason."

"I shan't give you a reason. You'll understand in good time." He turned away and tied a bow tie with great care, then brushed his fine black hair and added scent to his armpits before he buttoned his shirt. "I'll be back this afternoon. I'm going to be busy this morning. You may order lunch to be sent up. Order whatever you like."

After he left, Cyri tried on all her clothes and posed before the mirror till she was weary. At one o'clock she ordered a bountiful lunch and when the boy stepped into the room, she asked him something that had been puzzling her all morning.

"Why do you suppose it's all right for me to be naked before him and not before you?"

The boy started, turned crimson and averted his head. "Mebby it's because he's your father."

Cyri might have given away secret information at that point because the words rose to her lips to deny that Beverly was her father, but for some reason she chose not to reveal their relationship. She was not exactly proud of him and she didn't care to have others know about the previous night's performance, although the thought sent a hot reaction through her.

"We will go out tonight," said Beverly as they finished dinner in the Cobalt Room of the Berryland-East Hotel. It had been a delicious meal, served faultlessly, but the girl had not enjoyed it. First, there had been stares when she walked in, preceding Beverly to their table. The stares troubled her because for the first time, she felt strange and self-conscious in her new clothes. That their fit and expensiveness had caused the stares with keen attention to the elegant torso that wore them never entered her simple mind. She stripped off the white gloves which she did not like because they were hot, and before he could stop her, had snatched off the thirty dollar hat and gave her head a fierce shake like a filly that had just been unbridled.

"Why did you do that?" he asked in a fierce whisper.

"Because I don't like hats. I've never liked hats and I'll never wear one again."

"You'll wear what I tell you," he said with careful accents, "when I tell you, and in what manner I tell you."

She slowly focussed her great green eyes on him, and mimicking his careful enunciation, said, "I'll wear what you tell me, unless you happen to tell me to wear that horrible hat again. If you do, I'll refuse to do it."

Beverly drew a quivering breath, and at that moment realized the limitations of his power over the girl. There were few reactions which she shared with other girls he had discovered, and he scarcely knew how to take her.

Beverly's strange urges had led him into many and devious experiences, avoiding the type of men whom he resembled and was invariably taken for, arranging for the gratification of his appetites elsewhere.

To Cyri he was neither this, that, nor the other. She knew that Beverly was not like her father, T'Cal or Shem, but she did not accept his strangeness as anything out of the ordinary. She knew that her life had been severely restricted in scope as well as in learning. Her schooling had been sporadic, and she had had to quit at an early age that she might work for sufficient food to keep her young body in strength and health. She had always been an avid reader and a great admirer of lords and ladies, heroes and heroines in the books. Much of what she read she could not turn to personal advantage simply because she could not find anything approaching real life counterparts. She knew this from reading ... that there was much that she did not know. This vital bit of wisdom made her accept as no more than natural many things that would have balked a more cosmopolitan person.

The meal was an ordeal because Beverly, in low tones, severely criticized her eating habits, pointing out that ladies do not push food onto their forks with their thumbs, and was pardonably irritated when she asked, "Why?"

Beverly floundered for a moment, not being able to think of any good reason except, "Never mind why. Ladies simply do not do such things, and for God's sake, wipe the gravy from your lips."

She removed the gravy not by wiping but by licking. "That keeps from wasting the gravy," she said in apologetic expatiation while Beverly groaned.

He felt as though he had been beaten when he left the dining room, and felt worse when the head waiter came toward them and patted Cyri on the shoulder. "You must come again," he said in a kindly voice. "I could tell that you enjoy good food."

Cyri smiled at him sweetly. "Thank you," she said. "The food was very good and we will come again."

Beverly, who was no exception to the rule, felt somewhat over-awed by the head waiter—a type of person employed to over-awe people. He grinned a sickly sort of grin. "Thanks … we'll come again."

The head waiter ignored him and patted the girl's shoulder again before turning away and devastating a gaping underling with a cold gaze.

"What a nice man," said Cyri as they stepped into Canal Street.

"A hired hand," snarled Beverly, stung to the quick by the attitude of the man and a subtle certainty that Cyri realized that he had been put in his place. He was subconsciously giving the girl credit for occult powers and was becoming even more irritated without knowing the exact cause.

"We will now go to a bar," announced Beverly. "I know a place where we can get private rooms."

Cyri, who was enjoying the walk, people, shop windows and the tall buildings said, "I like bar rooms."

"I didn't ask whether you liked bar rooms," he barked testily.

"I know … I just said I like them. People get happy in bar rooms."

"People get drunk in bar rooms," he reminded her.

"Is that why you're going?"

"It is not why I'm going," he said with an exaggerated show of patience. "I'm going ..." He stopped short. He could not tell her in so many words why he was going to the bar, so he wisely kept his mouth shut. It wasn't safe to open it too freely in her presence. She did not pursue the subject, being interested in the street cars and traffic cops at whom she waved. They waved back to Beverly's intense mortification.

"They're nice men," she said. "They speak to you."

"With you waving your hand in their very faces, what else could they do?"

"They could turn their heads and look some place else."

Beverly felt like screaming but he did not. They got his car from the parking lot, and drove across Canal Street into the Vieux Carré.

"The bar is a few doors down," he said. "We'll walk the rest of the way."

The girl was watching a sunset that held her rapt attention and she didn't hear him.

"I said get out, we're here."

She waved a slim brown hand at him. "Be quiet, I'm listening to the sunset."

Beverly blinked. "You're doing what?"

"I'm listening to the sunset ... Listen, can't you hear it?"

"Sunsets," he said carefully, spacing his words, "make no sound."

"That's silly," she retorted easily. "I can hear it ... the most beautiful music in the world ... that is, besides Gene Autry."

Beverly laid hold of his senses, figuratively, with both hands, "Yes ... yes ... I'm sure, but let's go."

"No, I'm going to stay here till it fades and I can't hear it any longer. You go ahead."

"I'm not going ahead," he said, losing his temper. "You're coming and you're coming now. Listening to the sunset, indeed ... what rot!" He caught her wrist and attempted to drag her past the driver's seat to the street, but he failed. Bracing herself against the steering wheel, she surged backward, causing Beverly's head to strike the top of the car with enough force to cross his eyes. When he blinked away the tears and looked at her again, she had her chin propped on her knees which she had elevated, listening to the sunset. From where he stood, he could see the smooth lines of her thighs with their dusky tanned elegance, as could the meanest denizen of the Vieux Carré, had he been looking.

"Pull your dress ... For God's sake, cover your nakedness ... Do you want to get us arrested?"

She languidly complied without speaking or taking her eyes from the magnificent sweep of blues, pinks and exotic crimsons marbled against the western sky.

Beverly reeled against the side of the car, mopped his face with a snowy handkerchief, and turned over in his mind the girl's outrageous ignorance, stubbornness, and her extreme attractiveness which made every other girl he had ever known pale into the vaporous smog of nothingness. Apparently the sundown symphony had grown too dim for her to hear, so she came smiling from the car, stepping with what appeared to be graceful delicacy, but what was in reality common caution due to the extreme height of her heels.

They walked into the bar with Cyri standing target for thirty-odd stares which affected her as had those at the Cobalt Room. Temperamental discomfort was something to which she was ill-accustomed, and she despised standing there while

Beverly talked to the immense man behind the bar. Cyri looked at him because he seemed to be the least offensive man in the place. His face was broad and his chins receded with disappearing frequency into the neck of his florid, open-necked sport shirt, reminding her of two facing mirrors she had seen the day before and their innumerable reflections that gradually grew into nothingness. She could sense kindness and understanding behind his wall of flesh, and she admired the way he seemed completely at home without appearing to know that there were any people in the place, save when they tendered him a check in payment for drinks.

Beverly came back and together they walked up the stairs to the tiny room in which were a table, several comfortable chairs and a small lounge. Beverly took the tray from Willie at the door, trying to prevent the colored man from entering, but the moment his back was turned, Willie pushed into the room, arranging chairs by the table, puttering busily but uselessly about, smiling at Cyri, and taking in everything.

"I hope everything will be comfortable," he told Cyri, ignoring Beverly, as had the head waiter at the Cobalt Room.

"It's very nice," said Cyri, taking Willie's interest as a bid for friendship … which, of course, it was.

"I've seen better," sniffed Beverly contemptuously, only to be further ignored.

"Thank you, ma'am," said Willie, bowing low and casting an infuriatingly enigmatic glance at Beverly as he left the room. The door slammed forcibly shut and Willie grinned as he walked down the stairs.

"Why is it that you always manage to get into conversation with tradespeople and other such low stratas of humanity … cops … head waiters … nigger bar swabs?"

"What makes them low stratas of humanity?" she asked.

Beverly opened his mouth, cursed having opened it, swallowed, and breathed deeply. "Were you so closely reared that you do not recognize the difference between individuals?"

"What do you do?" she asked.

"I'm a salesman for matches … advertising matches … matches they give away at restaurants, bars, and filling stations."

"And does that make you better than head waiters?"

"Infinitely."

"How?"

The man almost shrieked with exasperation, but clamping his lips tight, he poured a generous portion of schnapps and sloshed ginger ale into the glass, adding ice.

"Would you like a drink?" he asked, carefully modulating his voice.

She smiled. "Of course. I wondered when you'd ask me."

With a crafty look on his face, he poured a heavy portion of the liquor into a glass and added ginger ale. She tasted it and enjoyed the minty alcoholic burn as it slid past her tonsils to puddle in her stomach, making a warm spot like a kitten curled up sleeping. She drank it faster than she should and before she was through munching the ice, she felt very light, like she might leave the floor and soar about without power like a balloon.

After the second drink, she left the table to lie down on the couch, putting her feet up on the back. She wriggled in pure sensual joy, completely released by the heady burn of the alcohol. Her dress slipped up exposing the white briefs stretched with such delicious tautness over her middle. Beverly downed his drink and eyed the unblemished quality of her skin, the carefully contrived curves of her long legs.

"There seems to be any number of things you can't explain to me," she said, comfortably wrigging deeper into the soft upholstery of the divan.

"You're too young and uneducated," he said, surprised at his own frankness, also beginning to feel released by drink. "However, you speak very well for someone who is so palpably ignorant."

"I've read a lot," she admitted, "and lots of people used to correct me, like Father Francioni, Mr. Leatherstone, the principal of the school ... and I went through the third grade."

"Come over here and take my clothes off," he commanded.

"Stay over there and take off your own clothes."

Beverly bit his lip. At first she had been very cooperative, now she was turning into a stubborn, willful girl who had a flair for asking upsetting questions. Beverly almost wept from baffled rage and started to take off his shoes.

"Will you undress yourself?"

"Yes, if you want me to."

"No, no, no," he interjected hastily. "Don't do it ..." He looked cautiously around, then turned to the girl as she lay unresisting on the couch, her green eyes on him, her breath coming faster as she thought of the night before. The occasional touch of his hands wrung slight starts from her as her skin grew so sensitive that the touches were like the breath of a hot iron.

Finally, when she lay still, apparently relaxed, supine, tawny and as smooth as peach down, supple and sinewy as a dancer, Beverly's heart swelled to the bursting. He traced her outline with slim delicate fingers and tasted the tips of her, as though drinking from fragile ceramic fountains.

In spite of the storms of almost paralytic ecstasy that swept her, the girl was conscious of the lack of something ... something missing from an otherwise perfect picture ... something that had to do with the revulsion which threaded its way even through the pink clouds of dreamy collapse. It was over and her skin tingled from the rough contact of his slight growth of beard. Weak from muscular contraction, emotional fatigue, and regression from the peak of alcoholic stimulation, she slept.

Behind the ornate bar, a bar of another time, a bar which shone with a polish of the same unbelievable brightness which sometimes adorns the shoes of a particularly snappy Leatherneck, sat three hundred and fifteen pounds of Acy Jones. Acy's stool was in no way related to the stools one often sees in bar rooms because his had been constructed by a genius with an electric arc who had considerable knowledge of strength of materials and strut bracing. It was constructed from the same material as one sees in the fuselage of airplanes and so put together that it would have supported a much greater weight than now sat upon it. In front of Acy was one of the oldest types of nickel-plated gingerbreaded cash registers which sounded, when in operation, much like a fast passenger train hurtling at high speed through a maze of switches ... complete with bell effects. In front of him was a bowl of peeled boiled eggs, an ancient cut glass bowl that might now command a fantastic price due to its extreme age and jewel-like decor. In another less pretentious bowl was a heap of rye wafers and in his fat and yet dainty hand was a container somewhat less in volume than a nail keg, containing dark beer ... possibly bock.

"Nnnn-f-f-f-f," sniffed Acy wriggling his nose. "Willie."

"Yes, sir," answered the little colored man who was assiduously applying wax to the further end of the bar.

"Take this egg back to the kitchen and tell Daisy that she has parboiled one of God's living creatures. Tell her that when I want chicken I prefer one not imprisoned in a wall of shell."

Willie grinned and continued to polish. Complaint came to Acy in the same way that life-giving air found its way into his nostrils. It was just a part of Acy.

"Gonna have a good day to-day, Willie," said Acy, running a long tongue out and removing a deposit of suds from his upper lip.

"Yes, sir," replied Willie. "The omens are good and the times propitious."

Acy grunted and heaved his bulk in a quarter circle, the better to glower at his aide. "There ye go agin, making me feel like an illiterate ... who'd you say taught you such good English?"

Willie swelled visibly. "Mister George Walker Everettson, the Third. A gentleman and a scholar of the what we might call a stratospheric order."

"Napf-f-f-f," Acy had a variety of noises which indicated various things like joy, dismay, dislike, irritation, and other emotions. The last was a composite bit of onomatopoeia. It combined irritation and dismay. Acy's own fund of His Royal Majesty's spoken tongue had increased something like three hundred percent since Willie had come to work for him ten years ago, but the fact rankled somewhat and he usually greeted Willie's windy discourses with mingled emotions.

Two men came into the bar, the first customers of the day. One walked to the further end of the bar while the smaller of the two came directly up to Acy, producing a revolver and shoving it uncompromisingly at the fat man. "This here is a stick-up, Guts," he said grittily. "Hand over the lucre."

Sudden silence from Willie's end of the bar indicated that he was similarly engaged, so Acy smiled ingratiatingly. "We serve a wide variety of mixed and unmixed drinks, stranger. What's your choice?"

The rat faced little man's face grew rattier and harder. "A kale sandwich and four mugs of silver, Guts, and no more yebber about what you serve ... get it?"

"The gentleman," said Willie softly from the other end of the bar, "displays a lack of learning and does brutally inefficient things to the language. I can maintain an excellent stand here, sir, should you ..."

With a lightening like move, Acy's right hand shot out and with a heave that spoke eloquently of more than fat, plucked the fellow over the bar as he might a sofa pillow and hurled him into a stack of empty prop bottles under the mirror. With speed scarcely abated, another bottle descended with shattering force on the hapless one's head. A glance toward the end of the bar showed Willie pointing the other's gun in his chest. He, in his turn, had taken advantage of the reciprocal diversion. "Warlike moves now severely contraindicated," he breathed softly. "I should say, Mr. Jones, that we have accomplished a double diversion which has successfully bilked the bandits."

"Alliteration," snorted Acy who now descended from his stool and, picking up his personal victim, hurled him bodily back over the bar where he struck the sawdust floor with a thud. "Alliteration," complained Acy again. "It gets even you."

"It has an almost irresistible magnetism at times," said Willie humbly. "I apologize."

Acy waddled to the end of the bar and picked up a phone, dialed, spoke briefly to the police, and cradled the receiver. "Gimme the gun, Willie."

Carefully watching the man, Willie complied.

Acy leaned over the bar and with a quick wrist-whipping motion brought the barrel down on the fellow's head and grunted with satisfaction as he crumpled up on the floor. "Stupid people, coming in here, giving me heartburn ... A nuisance and an imposition. One o' these days I'm gonna get mad."

"One can see," opined Willie, gently, "that you are even now respectably irritated."

Acy shrugged and walked back to the cash register where he pulled himself laboriously up on his stool. "Nuf-f-f-f ... Goddamn imposition ... irritation ..."

"Enough," put in Willie, preparing to replace the broken bottles, "to produce an uneven approach to the exigencies of the day's labor."

Acy slurped up a sufficiency of beer and washed his mouth out ... swallowed, and salted another egg. "Imposition, that's what. By the way, tell Daisy that all ye have to do to boil an egg is to put it into water and boil rapidly for fifteen minutes. It is not necessary to petrify them."

"I suggest that you tell her," said Willie sucking a fore-finger where a sliver of glass had entered unbidden. "Daisy is not in the best of temper these days ... you tell her."

Acy shook his head. "Might hurt her feelin's."

"Might mention, sir, in that event I should fare much worse than would you."

Acy grunted and returned to his eggs and beer, muttering about the discommoding matter of having to associate with a talkative as well as an educated smoke.

The police came, led by a bored sergeant whose feet obviously pained him considerably, took the men into custody and departed with them, seeming to appreciate the fact that Acy was in a bilious mood and not up to light badinage.

When Beverly Babcock walked into the bar and asked for a private booth, Acy was both offended and curious. He was not uninformed as regards such men as Beverly who might be classed as one of spurious masculinity, all the way from his first name to the limp wrists and languid gestures, but never in all his fifty years of experience had he seen one who was accompanied by a beautiful girl of immature years, nor one who desired alcohol in large quantities. Usually they stayed sober, the better to duck infuriated swings which they gathered in numbers, unless they operated among their own ilk.

Beverly minced to the bar and tendered a personal card with the flourish of a British club patron. "I desire a private room for the young lady and myself," he announced breezily. "I understand that you have means of gratifying my desires."

Acy picked up the card and glanced at it. Then he gazed at Beverly with clear amber eyes for an uncomfortable space of time. "Yeah ... I got what you want. That'll be ten dollars, exclusive of drinks and service."

With a shrug that meant to register contempt but which, in reality, only amounted to a wriggle, Beverly produced a fat roll and handed over the amount. "I shall require service only when I ring for it," he said grandly. "You may send up a quart of Peppermint Schnapps and a magnum of ginger ale ... with ice."

Acy almost gagged, but managed to nod his head. "It'll be up right behind you." He turned to Willie as Beverly led his lady out of sight. "You hear what that swish ordered?" Willie nodded.

"O.K., take it up. Glad I ain't got to repeat it." He shuddered.

"Glad you *don't have* to repeat it."

"That's what I said," retorted Acy puffing and turning red.

"Not precisely." Willie picked up his set and departed.

For the next thirty minutes Acy was too busy using the noisy cash register to think, and when business slacked up, he sat back and burped delicately behind a pink, moist palm. "Willie, tell Daisy to boil me a bowl of eggs."

Willie sighed, looked at his employer discreetly, and coughed behind his hand.

Acy snorted and heaved about. "Don't tell me you're afraid to deliver my order."

"It's not that, sir … it's about that couple in number seven. That gentleman is a most unsavory appearing character."

"We get a lot of unsavory characters in this place … bar's lined with 'em right now … since when did you get partickler … er, particular."

"It's not that exactly … not the man I mean. The little girl, sir, is a great lady."

"Papf-f-f-f … how'n hell you know that? If she's such a great lady, what's she doin' with him?"

"Submit, sir, that you have been dropping your 'g's' to-day more than usual."

"Go to blazes, and answer my question."

"It is hard to say, sir. One gathers these things sometimes through the operation of one's unconscious mind … without being in exact possession of the mechanics of the …

"Bushwa," snarled the fat man. "You and your book learnin'. I asked you what you suppose she's doin' with him?"

Willie shrugged eloquently. "Such questions are hard to answer. My position now is far removed from the day when you found me about to disintegrate my honor, pride and self respect by digging a half eaten flounder from your garbage disposal container."

"It was a perfectly good flounder," said Acy defensively. "I had expected mackerel which I relish highly …" He paused to let the sound of this rather neatly turned phrase tickle his tongue and ears, "… and when Daisy put this flounder before me, which was a perfectly good fish mind you, only I do not relish it as highly …"

"I understand," said Willie, attempting to stem the rush of talk, "that you prefer mackerel to flounder. I merely wanted to point out that digging into garbage is a demeaning act and eroding no end to one's pride. This child could have come to her present dilemma in some similar and entirely blameless manner."

Acy, somewhat offended by the interruption when his tongue was working smoothly, turned around and sulked a little while Willie went to deliver the order to Daisy. Acy thought also that things must be coming to a strange pass when men like Beverly turned to girls like … whatever her name was. That she was very young was displayed in her eyes, her carriage, and the petal smooth quality of her skin. It had been exposed considerably to sunlight and the soft nut brown thus produced made Acy's mouth water. The girl's body was almost developed, slim, yet sufficient, suggestive of great activity and freedom of movement. Her legs were long and looked hard and conditioned without being knotty, her clothes though new and in good taste seemed to fit her suspiciously as though they were not in tune with her personality except in the area where her young breasts punched the material into conical tents and made it accept the condition. Acy opened his hands and looked at the sweat glistening in them, rubbed them on the legs of his trousers and, with a sigh of irritation, slid from his stool.

Willie, coming back from his errand, collected several orders, then faced his boss. "You'll take a look?"

"Yeah … not because of what you said, though … remember that."

Willie smiled, showing perfect white teeth. "Of course not … perish the thought."

"Glau-f-f-f-" snarled Acy, and brushed by the colored man, feeling the smile in his back as he made his way aft and entered his private elevator.

CHAPTER THREE

—ACY

ACY MOPPED his streaming brow and squdged his hands together, feeling the dripping sweat and the soft thickness of palmar skin. He ran a finger inside his collar and, walking to his elevator, emitted a tremendous whoosh! Acy was some thing of a peeping Tom and had seen many things through his little Judas windows. It was a form of entertainment of which he never tired and he had had many deeply satisfactory belly laughs from what he saw. This was another matter. In all his watching, he had never seen so divine a human female, none that could even suggest that on the same sort of human bones he'd ever see so delightful an arrangement of flesh, such superb quality of comformity, of skin and of facial beauty.

He emerged at the floor of the bar and waddled back to the cash register where he rang up a number of sales placed on the counter nearby by Willie. He heaved himself up on his stool, salted a boiled egg and crammed several rye wafers into his mouth.

"Brimme a schooner o' suds, Willie ... bock."

Willie took the huge container and emptied a number of bottles of bock into it, bringing it back and placing it before the big man. "You saw?" he suggested.

Acy nodded heavily. "Never want to see nuthin ... er, nothing like that again ... Don't never ..."

"Ever," corrected Willie, gently.

"Ever," snarled Acy grumpily. "Don't ever let him in here again."

"A laudable resolution," agreed the black man with an understanding nod, "but the girl …"

Acy swallowed half an egg and almost choked washing it down hurriedly with a huge draught of bock. "The gal … whut about her?"

"I gathered that she had impressed you as she had me."

"She let 'im," growled Acy regretfully. "Never raised a hand. She stays out, too."

Willie raised a pair of gimlet black eyes to Acy's, so steady that it was like being struck in the face with wet gloves. "May I pose a theoretical array of conditions which could possibly account for her acquiescence? I am never wrong about potential ladies and gentlemen, no matter what surface manifestations might appear."

Acy wriggled uncomfortably. "Sure, pose away."

"I submit that she might have been a young girl, reared by him. Niece, distant relative, or maybe she is no relation … just a ward. He could have trained her or, if I am incorrect in this, I can think of innumerable other possibilities. It occurs to me that we are not so replete with ladies and gentlemen that we can allow one to escape and gradually sink to a depth from which there is no arising."

"Well, what the hell, what can I do?" Acy was on the defensive. "Walk up to him and say, 'Hey, you … you … !'," Acy stopped. He was at a loss to pin a name on Beverly because he had turned out to be something with which Acy had had no experience, either personally or in any of his voluminous reading. He gulped and continued. "Walk up and say … Hey, you, I want that there girl … that girl, I mean?"

Willie shook his head. "No, sir. If you undertook activity in so blunt a manner, I dare say you'd fail. There have been other occasions when I was rather amazed at the shrewdness of your thought processes." Willie smiled and went to answer a summons at the bar.

For two hours Acy wrestled with himself and repeatedly said both aloud and to himself, that this was none of his business, if people chose to act as those in Number Seven had, then who was he to say nay! Fifty times he shrugged his shoulders for the last time, and fifty times the sight of the girl on the couch came back to him causing a knot to rise in his throat, choking him with gentle insistence and making his eggs as dry as seared leaves. Beer had to be dumped down in flagons to dissipate them and when it was nearly time to close, he crashed his schooner down on the bar startling one sleepy drunk and frightening three more. The latter three took the interruption as their leave to go, but the fourth was too owl eyed and confused, so he poured out another glass of beer and drank it noisily. Willie, who recognized the symptoms, grinned toothily and in response to the master's nod, politely but firmly assisted the drunk to the door and ejected him, accomplishing it so neatly that the man shook hands with him three times and called him "stout feller."

Willie locked the door, noting as he did that Beverly and his companion were coming down the stairs. The girl had a numb look in her eyes, her face drawn and not too good in color. He marched to the bar and flipped a twenty dollar bill on the bar.

"Take it out of there," he said stiffly. "The man was impertinent, therefore, he does not receive the customary honorarium."

"Ummm," grunted Acy ringing the register and handing the change over the bar. "What'd he do?"

"He came in against my wishes and...." Beverly stopped and cudgeled his brain for some good stinging reason, "... and spoke to my er ... daughter."

"That was bein' ... being impertinent?"

"Certainly. I desire service from menials and nothing else. Might help if you'd remember that in the event I ever decide to come back."

Acy climbed slowly from his stool and seemed to grow hard, to lose his flaccid pose of sleepiness. "You ain't gone yet," he pointed out.

Beverly pocketed his change. "I'm going now."

"That, m'boy, is what you think."

Beverly was appalled and hardly believing. "What ...? Are you mad ...? Of course I'm going. Come along, Cyri."

Cyri lingered a moment. "The colored man didn't do anything, sir. He's lying."

Acy grinned affably. "I was sure of it, Sugar."

Beverly, fairly smoking with rage, reached the door and found it locked. He grew a shade paler. "This portal is locked."

"Right," agreed Acy, heartily. "It's locked. So you don't seem to be going after all."

The little man flew into a hysterical funk and wheeling around tore at the door with both hands, kicking and screaming with fright. The longer he fought, the noisier and more hysterical he became, until at last he reeled away from the door and sat heavily in a chair and began to sob wretchedly. Cyri, who had watched his antics with interested contempt, turned, walked to the bar, and pulled herself up on a chair facing Acy.

"Please, may I have an egg ... I'm hungry."

Acy looked into the clear depths of her jade eyes and sighed. He didn't understand, but he was about ready to agree with

Willie. Behind two such magnificently honest eyes there could be nothing of a vicious, sinful nature.

"Sure, Sugar." He shoved the bowl to her. "Willie, get the gal a glass … no, a pint of milk and tear up a few pieces of French bread, butter it and toast it. Jump, dammit, she's hungry."

"I don't care what Mr. Beverly said, he's a nice man … Willie, I mean."

"Sure he is," agreed Acy. "Mister Beverly … he said you was his daughter."

She shrugged lightly. "Yes, that's what he told the people at the hotel. I'm not his daughter. I killed my father and had to leave River Oaks and he picked me up."

"You …" Acy managed to get some beer down before strangling. "You did what?"

Cyri looked at him with such calm seriousness that he felt undressed. "You won't tell anyone? They might want to take me back and hang me or … something."

Acy swallowed noisily. "No, I won't tell."

"I didn't think so … you seem to be such a nice man. Yes, sir, I killed him."

"What for?" breathed the fat man, leaning forward.

"Because he got in bed with me and tried to …" As she had done the sheriff, she told him in simple, blunt terms what her father had tried to do.

Acy picked up a bar towel, got it to his face, sniffed, and threw it down with a curse. He picked up a fresh one and wiped his streaming face. "Well, Sugar … can't say as I blame you."

She told him of her early life, of her mother's death, of T'Cal and Shem and the others. She bared her unsophisticated heart with such complete freedom that often Acy's cheeks were as wet with tears as they were with sweat.

"So," she concluded, "I had to get work here so they wouldn't hang me."

"Who said they'd hang you, Sugar," he almost whispered.

She pondered a moment, sliding a tendril of soft, black hair behind her ear. "No one, I guess ... but isn't that what they do to murderers?"

"That is called justifiable homicide," said Willie, who had miraculously accomplished his mission and still had not missed a word, as he put a platter of golden toast before her.

"What the smoke means," put in Acy, didactically, "is ..."

"Oh, I can understand him very well," she interrupted. "He means I was justified in killing my father." Acy glared and aimed a clumsy blow at Willie who, still giggling, skipped out of harm's way.

"I want to get out of here," whimpered Beverly, who had recovered somewhat and had bound up his bleeding fingers with two handkerchiefs. "You have no right to hold us here like this ... prisoners ... peonage ... kidnapping."

"Shaddup," growled Acy, "or I'll add murder to that long list of evil doings."

Beverly beat the heel of one hand tenderly on the table. "But why are you doing this ... why? I've never done anything to you. I paid my bill ..."

"Open the door, Willie, and let him go," said Acy, frowning. "No, not you, Sugar," he put a restraining hand on her arm. "You can stay here with us."

Her eyes grew wide and she swallowed a mouthful of food. "Gee ... you mean I can stay here ..."

"You can till we find something for you to do."

"I refuse to leave without her ... she is my, ah, ward."

"I don't think she is anything of the kind, Petunia. I think you picked her up on the road and I know what went on in the room tonight. I took a picture of it … you didn't notice, probably. You was otherwise occupied … so run along or I'll call the police and we'll see what they have to say about it."

Beverly went white and scuttled out of the door which Willie held open for him, bowing low as he went through the portal.

"Go ahead, kid, and eat up. We get up late here, so it's a long time till breakfast."

She had grown still and her appetite was gone. She shoved the food away. "I'm … not hungry any more."

"O.K. We'll have a good breakfast for you in the morning."

"Shall I prepare the guest room for the princess?" asked Willie, with a low bow that brought a trembling smile to the girl's lips.

"Nnnuf-f-f," snorted Acy. "'Sif you haven't already done … did …"

"Done is correct, Sir."

"Go to hell," bellowed Acy, turning red in the face. He puffed loudly and turned to the girl. "Sugar, did you have any clothes?"

Her lips trembled ever so slightly. "Yes, sir, but they're all at the hotel room in Mr. Beverly's …"

"Never mind … Oh." A slow grin flitted over Acy's broad face. "Let's wait about fifteen minutes and see if my hunch is right and if it is … Come on, Sugar, and I'll let you ride the elevator with me."

Acy's big living room was furnished in solid, splendid comfort. There were deep overstuffed chairs, two magnificent divans as soft as down, a black bear skin rug that was spread in front of the fireplace thrown over a deep blue carpet that was laid from wall to wall. On the walls were ancient rifles, three pairs of crossed dueling sabers, an old iron-studded Thibetan shield, three excellent Currier and Ives prints, and over the mantel was a richly colored portrait of a woman. It was this picture that drew the girl's attention over all the rest. Slowly she walked first to this side, then that, and finally, she walked directly to the mantel and placed her elbows on it and looked upward.

"Everywhere you go she still looks at you. I think she is very beautiful."

"The most beautiful woman that ever lived," said Acy, reverently, his voice cello-soft and vibrant with deep feeling. It caused her to look around and fix him again in the pincers of her direct gaze.

"You loved her very much, didn't you?"

Again Acy was struck by her penetration. There was no reason for her to assume that he had loved the woman, and yet, she sensed it immediately. "Yes, Sugar ... I loved her very much."

She continued to stare at him and again he noticed that her chin trembled and wondered why, because she did not impress him as being particularly emotional.

"Why did you take me from Mr. Beverly ... after you saw what happened in the room?"

Acy met her gaze steadily. "Because I don't like Mr. Beverly and I don't think it was right for him to do as he was doing."

She looked away for a moment, then back. "Yes, I suppose people would think it is wrong."

"Didn't you want to leave him?"

"Oh, yes, sir. I was beginning to dislike him a great deal. He bit me tonight."

Acy strove to maintain his composure. "You said that people would think what you did was wrong, didn't you think so?"

A tiny frown worried her forehead, and she was silent for a moment. "What is *wrong*, Mr. Acy?"

"Call me plain Acy, Sugar," he said and could go no further. A silence fell on the room and he could feel her eyes boring into him. Willie, seated on a footstool before the fireplace, murmured,

"From the mouthes of babes come forth Gordian knots. It will be highly edifying to see how you answer that, my master."

"Ah ... shut up that pseudo-humility, you second conscience ... Sugar, it might be better if you'd tell me what you consider to be right and wrong." He ignored a smothered noise from Willie and held her steady gaze. She sighed and pulled an ottoman close to his knees and rested her arms on them as though she had been accustomed to doing so all her life.

"Wrong is when you do something to someone that they don't like or maybe don't deserve."

"*Touché,*" muttered Willie, while Acy chewed his lower lip.

"Well, that much is correct and I'll tell you an old rule that people have been using for a couple of thousand years which, after all the arguing has been done, seems still to fit the bill better than any other. 'Do unto others as you would have them do unto you.' "

"That's the Golden Rule."

"Correct."

"Well, I've never done anything to anyone to hurt them, so why should people in River Oaks hate me? Why should my father want to do that to me when I didn't want him to, and why should Mr. Beverly bite me?"

Willie cleared his throat and looked fixedly at the far wall.

Acy squirmed in his chair. "What did you do in River Oaks to make people hate you?"

She told him frankly and in some detail. "It didn't concern them in the least. It was between T'Cal and I and it wasn't till he brought Shem around that things began to get bad. They found out and wanted to run me out of town. Father Francioni told me."

"What did he advise you to do?"

"He told me not to run until I had to."

"He didn't tell you that what you had done was wrong."

She shook her head. "He said that much unhappiness some-times came from such things, but he never told me that they were wrong."

"Now," said Willie, looking toward heaven, "I have heard everything."

Acy mopped his streaming face and snarled. "Turn on that hot damn fan.... I'm roasting."

Willie rose, grinning. "I, too, feel the impact of considerable temperature."

Acy got up and walked heavily to the phone and after look-ing up a number, dialed. "Hello, Berryland East?" He spoke in a falsetto voice, perfectly mimicking Babcock, making Cyri giggle. "This is Babcock ... just checked out and I find that in my rush, I left my daughter's clothes there. Will you have someone pack them and I'll send a colored man over to pick them up ... Yes, thank you."

He transfixed Willie with his colorless eyes. "The smoke I was speaking of is none other than Willie Sanderson ... git." ...

"Get," corrected Willie, mildly, as he left the room.

The girl giggled again. "He does you like Father Francioni used to do me."

"Yeah ... blinkin' plague, that smoke." He sat down again and she pulled her chair stool close again. "What will you do with me, Mr.... I mean, Acy?"

"Well, I'll let you stay here till ..." He stopped short. Her hands had clutched his knees.

"But I don't want to go any place. I like it here. I like you and I like Willie ... Please, Acy, I can work very hard." Her chin was trembling again and her story came to him afresh, pouring over him like a blanket of human accusation. His throat closed and stopped his voice.

"I ..." Two great tears trickled down his fat face, running crazily hither and thither as they ran into various creases. It happened without either of them knowing why, but of a sudden she was crumpled on his tremendous chest weeping stormy, bitter tears and Acy was holding her close, his own eyes dripping like worn faucets. For a long time she wept with bleak violence, purging her hungry little soul to the depths, digging up and rooting out years of poverty, mistreatment, starvation, insecurity and want of little things which her acquaintances possessed in abundance and she not at all. Her diaphragm twitched her lithe body occasionally for a long time after the freshet of tears had ceased, and finally she raised her head.

"I'm awfully sorry, Acy. I can't ever remember doing that before in my life. I didn't mean to be a sissy."

Acy had to clear his throat several times before he could trust it to speak. "Sugar, there's nothing better in the world for a sore heart than a good cry. Tears do not denote weakness, but rather a full heart. I heard an old man say once that he never trusted a man who couldn't cry. By that he meant that anyone who considered it a weakness hadn't gone into the mechanics of crying very deeply and were shallow people."

She was silent for a long time, cuddling against his chest like a child, then she up and asked, "Acy, there's so much I don't know ... Do you think I'm bad?"

He cleared his throat again. "Cyri, do you think you're bad?"

"No!"

"Then they ain't a single human bein' in all creation that can say you are. You may be young and unworldly, you may be mistaken and you may have been a wild weed since you had to grow up all by yourself, but bad? Nope, you ain't bad."

"Then if people don't think they're bad, they're not?"

"Didn't say that. A man might steal something that ain't his and make enough excuses to where he'd convince himself that in his case, at least, it was all right. You're different. The things you did you stood to lose the most, you were the one exposed to danger and disgrace, so if after all that you still don't think you did wrong, then who can say you did?"

"How do you mean I was the one who could have lost the most, been disgraced?"

Acy breathed deeply and clenched his jaws before speaking. "Remember what you told me about Shem and T'Cal?"

"Yes."

"Suppose they had made you have a baby?"

She clasped her hands and thought silently for a moment. "Then it's so."

"What?"

"I heard Jenny Leclarde say that once and I didn't believe it. It's true, that's how babies are made?"

"Yes, it's true … Say, Cyri, how much schooling did you have?"

"Just to the third grade."

"Then how come you talk so well?"

"Well, I read a lot of books … I'm crazy about reading and there were some kind men and women who used to help me when I worked at their houses."

"Splatf," Acy popped his lips. "Then you got some more readin' to do and I got the best library in the city, private, that is, and you'll see just how and where kids come from. You got to learn that what you do is one thing, but what you git caught doin' is another. What you did was dangerous because it might have ruined your health to have a child at your age and you couldn't have taken care of it. If it gets talked around that you're that sort, then you lose your reputation like you did at River Oaks. That's where the wrong of it comes in. Not so much what you do right at the time, but what society will think, and believe me, they can make it awfully hard on you if they've a mind to."

Her eyes grew darker. "Then T'Cal and Shem knew what might happen when they played with me, didn't they?"

"Ain't seen a boy their ages in my life what didn't."

She considered this for a moment. "Then they aren't good people at all."

"They ain't and nobody else like 'em. Any time a man puts a woman's future and happiness in jeopardy for an idle five minutes then he's a dog from way back."

"I think you're right," she agreed stoutly. "Why do you suppose they will do it?"

"Ain't nobody ever been able to figger it out, Sugar. They does and that's all there is to it, some, that is. I don't mean to put the idea in your head that there ain't no good men in the world. There are and plenty of 'em, except that a lot of 'em ain't recognized because they don't pay the proper sort o' gesture to things as they is suppose to be.... Just like you."

"If," she said, frowning, "I understand you, then those gestures are dishonest unless the person is really like that."

A deep bubble of mirth tumbled from the cavernous reaches of Acy's chest like the warning rumble of a geyser. "Sugar, you strickly said yourself a mouthful that time. The rankest sorta dishonesty, but the public demands it so we have to hand it to 'em. Just like goin' into a poker party and askin' t' get cheated."

She raised her head to him, her chin trembling again. "Please, sir, can't I stay here? No one ever talked to me like you have ... I ..." Tears tumbled over her soft cheeks as she bit her lips to keep them back.

He reached over and picked her bodily from the stool and placed her in his lap again. "You can stay here just as long as Ole

Acy's got a roof over his head … Just as long as body and soul stays together, and you'n me gonna have more fun than anybody because we're so much alike. You, cause you don't know no better and me, I done found out it's the best way to be."

With a hand as tender as a woman's, Acy spread the girl's masses of hair in a fan shape covering her shoulders in a blanket of silken glory and Willie, coming back from his mission, stopped in the doorway and held his breath. For a long time he stood there, the edges of his white teeth showing in a wistful smile.

eagerness that both were left amazed and a little breathless. The moon let through enough light so that he could tell from the expression on her face that matters were ripe for conquest, the same look that had been on Else Noppe's face six months ago, although afterward Else became frightened and ran to her mother with the story. The resultant furor ended in a well-bred free-for-all of words, and the guillotining of acquaintance between two families who had been friends for years.

Mary Jane snuggled close and whispered, "That was very nice, Rod."

"Sure," he agreed smugly, deliberately fondling the front of her dress. "This'll be better." In a manner that was far in advance of what his experience should have been, he soon had her palpitant under the treatment of his lips and her stifled gasp was music to his ears. He kissed her again and again, both being shaken to such an extent that from then on there was a flurry of activity, tiny little wails of acquiescent resistance, which was quickly replaced by movement, endearing jabber which meant nothing yet everything, then dead silence for a long time.

The next afternoon he called her. "Come on over," he said, conspiratorially. "My parents are gone."

"Mine are too," she giggled. "I'll be right over."

She came and brought with her an astounding proposition, interrupting what was intended to be a savage oral onslaught with a cool palm. "Hold it a minute, swifty. Suppose we discuss terms."

Rod, not a little nettled at the interruption, was also somewhat mystified. "Terms ... what kind of terms?"

"Well, as they say in books, let's lay it on the line. You want what I have, right?"

"Sure, but what's that got to do ..."

"I'm handy, I'm nice, and I'm willing, right?"

"Right, but I …"

"Very well, I play, you pay."

Rod sat down suddenly and eyed her with distaste. "This beats me. I thought all your kind were herded together down in the French Quarter."

She pouted. "Don't be like that, Rod. You know you have all the money you want."

"Sure I do, but Christ … buying it … just like that. I can't see it. I sure had you figured wrong."

She giggled. "You thought last night was the first time, didn't you? Well, it wasn't. I wasn't but twelve the first time. You must have thought I learned fast."

At the moment Rod was thinking too fast, consequently wasn't thinking much of anything.

She glanced down at him coyly. "I can be nice, Rod." She arched her back and threw her breasts into sharp definition and he noticed that she wore no restraint. An empty feeling attacked the pit of his stomach and desire began to grip him.

"But, Mary Jane … paying you …"

"Rod, you're acting young and unsophisticated. Men keep women in cars, clothes, apartments and think nothing of it. In fact, I don't want real pay, what I want is a little kitty on the side, just in case."

"In case of what?"

"Well, take last night. Did you protect me?"

"N-no. I don't like those things, it's just like …"

"I know what boys say," she interrupted, "but suppose I would get pregnant, could you get a hundred dollars, maybe more, if I was sick afterward to get rid of it? Without answering a lot of questions, I mean."

Rod gulped. "No, I don't suppose I could."

"So you see," she continued, "I need something to watch out for myself with. Can't you understand that?"

He brightened. "Sure, Mary Jane, I see what you mean now ... and I guess you're right."

She sat on the couch with him and snuggled up close. "It won't be much, Rod, just three dollars...."

His mouth against hers prevented more conversation and she threw her arms about his neck and forced her warm, soft body close to him. He raised his head and pushed her wild hair out of the way.

"Let's go up to my room."

She nodded eagerly. "All right ... let's hurry."

The sight of her generous curves which were now his without hesitation, froze him for a moment. Heretofore, Rod's experience had been confined to the dark, more often than not in the back seat of an automobile, and this was something entirely new. She came over to him and held him close, shivering while his hands slid like small eager rodents down the cleft of her fine back, then around to the front where they held her.

Alone in the house and without fear of arousing attention, Mary Jane let go the precocious but fierce extent of her lusty nature and dragged Rod forcibly with her. To his utter surprise, things came in perfect order and with perfect ease, and Rod discarded the automobile forever. With ease and comfort came latitude of operation he had never dreamed of, and Mary Jane, being a woman, did not have to dream of them, but performed as a daughter of Eve to whom such things are never a secret unless the mind has been unduly influenced by other forces.

That was the beginning and though Rod went to several universities, he always managed to flunk out, coming home and renewing the association. At the age of twenty, Mary Jane admitted that by placing a price on her body, she had been enjoying things which her improvident parents could never have provided for her, things which she intended to have at all costs. She pretended to them that an aunt who had always given her things also began giving her money, the aunt being a lady of rather easy virtue herself, actually having put the idea into the girl's head in the beginning. So her family, who never suspected that behind Mary Jane's pretty, calm countenance was a brain in action, never caught on, and when she thought Rod was old enough she told him. She had planned well and he kissed and complimented her.

"You were always ahead of your time, Mary Jane. Think of it, two years younger than me and even then you made me leap the hurdles to your own tune."

Her smile was sweetly enigmatic. "You enjoyed it, Rod, and you were rather backward even if you did have unlimited chances to learn that were denied me."

If Rod considered this a tacit admission that he knew women, he had a great deal to learn. After leaving the University of Missouri under a cloud, he refused to make any further effort to gain an education, being content to drink., race about in his convertible, visit Mary Jane in her bachelor apartment for which he was paying and otherwise disport himself, including excursions into other and newer fields of which Mary Jane knew nothing. It is conceivable that had she known, she would have smiled and said nothing because Mary Jane was not the sort to let hay go unmade on days when the sun shone brightly. So when he visited her on a particular Saturday night and had explored every inch of her lovely body, gratified as usual by her eager response, he had a surprise awaiting him.

It was one o'clock in the morning and they lay on the bed close enough to feel the warmth from their bodies. Rod lay very still, his muscles aching with the utter fatigue of repleteness that such activities produce, smoking a cigarette, watching the thin tendrils of smoke climb toward the ceiling.

"Rod?"

"Yes, honey chile."

"I'm going home tomorrow."

He rolled over and sat up. "What's the matter, did you get fired?"

"No, I quit."

"For Christ's sake, why? I can't give you any more money. Pop's been sort of hard to get along with lately."

"I'm going to be married, Rod."

He laughed. "Well, that isn't so bad, is it? We can still meet some place. Whoever he is, you don't love him."

"No," she admitted, "I don't, but I've got something good now, Rod, and there'll be no meetings. This is the last time I'll see you."

Again he had laughed, very sure of himself and very smug about the whole thing. A week later, not having heard from her nor having seen her, he called her home.

In answer to his query, Mrs. Dallason drew a sharp breath. "Why, didn't she tell you she was getting married, Rod … Oh that *girl!* She was married Sunday afternoon and left by air Sunday night for Europe."

"Holy….," he stopped and clenched his jaws tightly for a moment. "Whom did she marry, Mrs. Dallason?"

"Wait till I write that girl," swore her mother. "She married Abel Dickinson, the sugar man from Cuba."

Rod swore silently to himself and thanking her, hung up.

Drink, which had started merely as a lark to Rod, now achieved the stature of a necessity and after an especially rough Saturday night, got in his car about noon Sunday and drove out to Ponchartrain Beach, there to soak out some of the fumes in the hot sun. For an hour he lay supine, feeling the hive of bees in his stomach quiet to a faint buzz. He sat up and looked dizzily about, scraping the sweat from his belly and trying to shake the bells from his ears. His mouth tasted like straw from a cat's bed and he rose with the idea of slaking his thirst with a beer.

The beer was immediately driven from his mind by the sight of a female striding across the beach, evidently headed for the soft drink stand. She wore a pale green suit that, had it not covered her buttocks so well, might have been tabbed as the Bikini type and so closely did it fit that it appeared to have been applied with a lipstick brush. She was long and so cleanly curved that Rod remembered to breathe only by the sheerest reflex. Her skin, a rich cream tan and apparently without a single flaw, fitted over her fully fleshed body without a wrinkle, as smooth as lacquered satin. It had the pinkish undertones and the dull oily sheen of superb health and her free stride betokened an uninhibited nature. Beneath the fragile bra, her full firm breasts rose honey brown about their bases and he knew that they'd be white as they neared their exciting pink tips.

Lengthening his stride and combing his hair as he went, he caught up with her as she stopped at the Coke counter, cocking one clean-cut leg on the rail asked for a drink.

"I," he said, modulating his voice carefully, "will consider it a privilege if you will allow me to pay for it."

She smiled winsomely, without the slightest hint of shyness. "All right, the privilege is yours."

CHAPTER FIVE
—THE PRINCESS

N THE TWO YEARS that Cyri had been with Acy many things had happened. Looming large among these was the matter of Acy's weight which had fallen from three-fifteen to a paltry two-eighty. His eggs were eaten in twos and threes now, instead of by the bowlful, and the size of his beer schooner had shrunk until it was no bigger than his fist, although this was still a fair sized mug.

Acy sat at his cash register and let his eyes wander over a full house. Times were good and when times were good, people drank the kind of drinks he sold. When times were bad they drank also, in order to make believe that times were good. Against his will, he had to admit that he felt better than he had in years. His step had a spring to it now and he felt less like a mountain and more like a man. He beckoned to Willie.

"Tell Daisy to boil me a bowl of eggs."

"Pardon," said Willie respectfully, almost offensively so, "but I have orders that you may have three eggs in the morning and four in the afternoon, Daisy," he continued hastily, trying to avert a threatened explosion, "is in collusion with the Princess and since I have to sleep with the former, I dare not carry out any contrary orders. Said dark female at present tips scales only a little below your honor."

"Fapppt," spurted Acy, "be darned if you ain't ..."

"Aren't," breathed Willie softly.

Acy eyed the dark man malignantly. "Yeah … damn if you aren't the talkative one to-day … where's Cyri?"

"At last account, she was engaged in altering your honor's trousers … the last pair, I think she said, and she seemed a bit irate that she had worked on selfsame trousers three times in the last two years."

"Serves 'er right," smirked Acy with a gleam of humor in his eyes. "All this here damn dietin'."

"The 'g,' " suggested Willie.

"The what … oh, yeah, the 'g.' "

"You were too engaged in pushing books into her adolescent hands," chaffed Willie. "So much so, that you inadvertently included one on diet and the dangers attendant to overt adiposity."

"Mummmp," Acy took the beer mug down and glanced longingly at the tap, but Willie shook his head.

Daisy was probably the same size no matter from what angle she was measured. Height, breadth and thickness were virtually the same, therefore she resembled nothing so much as a ball of dark suet. Her face shone with good nature and her bright eyes sparkled like freshly washed blackberries. She and Cyri bustled about arranging the dining room table in a festive manner, in the center of which was a cake of brobdinagian proportions with two tiny candles on it.

"Look like to me all this vittles gonna roon that diet," she said dubiously, reading over the menu.

"Let him have fun this once, Auntie. He's stuck with it so faithfully."

"But all dese aigs. He can't eat 'em wid all de res' o' this stuff."

Cyri smiled mistily. "They're just for looks and to let him know the roof's off. You can put them in the ice box and feed them to him as he should have them."

Daisy let her eyes rove over the girl as she polished a heavy silver fork with a paper napkin. "One sho' thing. You the fust woman er man whut ever made him quit all that eatin'. After Miss Celestine died, he went hawg wile."

"Poor Acy," the girl murmured. "He loved her so much, didn't he?"

"That he did. She was a fine woman. He didn't smile for a year after she died. He didn't live till you come cause he had done got so fat he couldn't hardly git 'round no mo'. De doctor tole him he didn't have long to live lessen he cut down eatin' and drinkin' all that beer."

The girl stopped polishing the silver and rested her steady eyes on the old woman's. "Daisy, what is love?"

Daisy laughed gustily, smiting her thigh. "There you got me. I done hear a lotta talk about it but ever body think it's diffunt. Now you take Willie. He stayed hyer fer near onto three years 'fo I ever looked at him twict. One night he come in mah room and say, 'Sis Daisy, me'n you livin' in the house ennyhow, so howcome me'n you don't stay in the same room. Hit'll save 'lectricity.' " She smiled to herself. "Lawdy, how dat man kin make love."

"You let him stay in the room with you?"

"Sho! I says, 'Willie, you done spoke whut Gawd love. Ain't a bit o' sense in burnin' two lights when one will do just as well, but I'm tellin' you if you stay in this room with me all night, you sho' gon' marry me in de mawnin'.' "

"Did he?"

"He sho did ... jes' like I say."

"But, Daisy, how did it feel."

Daisy shot her a curious glance. "How *whut* feel?"

"Love, how do you know when it's the real thing?"

"Oh ... well, I been in love fo', five times and they was all diffunt. Now Willie always made me feel like antses was crawlin' round in my clo'se. Oh, there was Cholly Red … that was when I was still up on the plantation. Cholly Red made me feel like somethin' was crawlin' round where didn't nuthin' have no business crawlin' round. Son Square … now dat was a love makin', long strangout, black nigger if ever one drawed breath. He made me feel like snails was crawlin' up mah legs and round and round … slow like. Sam Duncan was de ruffest and wildest. Dat man'd make me feel like a hoss had done kicked me … a reg'lar stud hoss, Sam was. Don't make no diffunce wheh love hit you, it always wind up in de same place."

Cyri smiled and began polishing the silver again. "I don't think so."

"How come?"

"Because … well, I'd been around a lot before I came here and … to tell the truth, I liked it a lot. I couldn't be truthful and deny it, but I wasn't ever in love with any of them."

"Oh, shucks, gal. I wasn't talkin' bout pleasurin'. I never was no tramp woman and I always picked my mens, but a good time is a good time. What's Saddy night fer if it ain't t' have a good time, but you jes' wait till one of 'em gits you *right*. You'll know de differunce. Well, dis ain't gettin' no vittles cooked … oh, one mo' thing. Honey, how come you ain't had nuthin' to do wid no man since you been hyer? It ain't healthy!"

Cyri sighed. "I don't know, Auntie. I suppose it's because I never go anywhere to meet them. Acy doesn't like for me to hang around in the bar."

"He plumb right. Ain't one man in fifty-five outa dat bunch o' trash what's any good. You oughta git out mo', go to the beach, make some friends. It ain't right fer a gal with de looks you got not to know no mens."

"Happy anniversary!" screeched Cyri jumping up and down as Acy lumbered through the door.

"Happy anniversary," screeched Daisy in her turn avoiding the gymnastics for good and sufficient reason.

"A multitude of the same," applauded Willie mildly, bringing up the rear.

The big man stopped short and breathed softly for a moment, looking at the table spread, the soft candle light reflecting in the rich gleam of the silver. The walls with their polished weapons and dull soft-toned paintings seemed to cast a halo of comfort and close homeliness over the room.

Acy wriggled his nose and sniffed audibly, looking acutely embarrassed. "Anniversary?" he croaked.

Cyri ran to him and drew him into her arms. "Two years, Acy ... two wonderful years I've been living with the dearest man in the world." Her eyes were damp and shining.

"Garuff," snorted the fat man, touching her hair with the tips of his fingers as Galahad might have touched the Holy Grail. His shyness seemed to leave him and his eyes were suspiciously moist. "Two years," he murmured with that resonant organ note in his voice which betokened deep feeling. "Two years of happiness, Sugar, when I never dreamed it would come again. I'll never be able to thank you enough for that."

"He didn't make a single grammatical error," whispered Willie to Daisy.

"What if he did?" she snapped back.

"Acy," said Cyri, "how can you say such a thing. You gave me this wonderful home and everything. And ..." she stepped back and lifting her arms high did a slow mincing pirouette, "... you didn't know it, but you gave me this dress too. I picked out the material and Daisy made it."

"I done the plain sewin'," said Daisy loyally. "All them plackets she put in herself."

A great throb of painful appreciation swelled in Acy's breast. There simply was no way to say in words how lovely she looked. At his request, she had always done her hair up in a very simple way, mostly consisting of brushing it back and letting it fall in deep soft waves to her shoulders. Tonight it gleamed in the rosy candle light like some fabulous metal with a deep inner fire that threw off a soft radiance seeming to generate its own voltage. The roof, nudeness, and a subtropical sun had kept her skin tanned with a master touch, never spotting, never coarsening, seeming to soak up life-giving rays to store and loose them through the mechanism of her personality which had come to life under Acy's expert guidance. She had lost all of her reticence and quiet stolidity. She blossomed as any human will under the lack of tension, the presence of a deep undemanding love, good food, lack of fear and full security.

It was a meal to be remembered from the standpoint of the quantity consumed by Acy, the excellence of its preparation, and the memories it evoked. Acy grinned so broadly that he gruffed and hid his face behind his napkin. He was thinking about the night Cyri, having bathed, went to her room only to find the heat duct closed and in attempting to open it had become chilled. Without a second thought about the matter, she had dashed into the living room where Acy sat reading. She was as naked as a banana but she was oblivious of it, and running to the fireplace, knelt before the blaze. Acy sat stunned, both from surprise and the sight she presented kneeling on the bear skin rug, the fire glinting rudily on her glowing skin, her breasts tight and sharp from the chill of the other room.

She turned and smiled at him without self-consciousness. "It was cold in my room," she said apologetically.

"Nuuufff," he barked eloquently. "Y'say it was, huh?"

"Yes, sir, the duct control is stuck." Suddenly she became aware that she was nude before a man and recalled that in some way it was supposed to be wrong. She rose slowly to her feet, her eyes stricken and dull with the expectation of disapproval. Tears rushed to her eyes and she said, "I'm very sorry, sir. I suppose I forgot, but somehow with just you in here I didn't ..."

"You didn't think it was wrong, did you, Sugar?"

"No, sir ... that is, it being wrong didn't impress me. I'm terribly sorry."

Acy rose to his feet. "Cyri," he rarely used her name, "set down on that rug and stay there till you get warm. By not thinking it is wrong to appear naked before me, you unconsciously pay me a great compliment. I appreciate it a lot. Never bother about me because you're like a daughter and yet, looking at you this way, I know I'll never see a lovelier body. It does something to me ... deep inside, something wonderful. It's like seeing an exquisite Chinese carving in the finest ivory, like a jade figurine turned out centuries ago by an artisan of unequaled skill."

Acy paused, rather amazed at the passion of his speech, nor was he alone conscious of it. Cyri looked at him for a moment, then ran to him and fell to her knees at his feet embracing his legs. His hand stroked the rich smoothness of her shoulders and back, marveling anew that into one woman nature could have put such classic bounty. She looked up, her eyes damp, a tremulous smile touching her lips.

"Acy, no one ever said such beautiful things about me before in all my life. Something inside just melted away."

His hands cupped her face as though he was examining a marvelous flower and tilted it slightly. "Sugar, you were born in the wrong place. They could see your beauty only as something to have for themselves and because of your poor station and an attitude they could never understand, they took what you gave, but yet they despised you because they could never understand you."

She sighed and rested her head against his knee. "I suppose other people have felt the same way, but someone who hasn't grown up the way I did can't even imagine what it was like ... and what it's like now that it's over with."

"Don't you think you should reconsider and go to school?" Acy asked this regretfully.

"Do you really want me to?"

"No, I don't."

"Then I won't go."

"Sugar, it's time you realized that I'm not keeping you here to order you around. By not wanting you to go to school I'm being selfish. Always remember that when decisions rest with you, you come first."

"I know that, Acy. I'm doing what I want to do. You want me to be around and because you want it, I want it too."

Acy felt a pang of fear. "But one of these days you'll meet some fine man who'll want to take you away from me. Naturally I'll want you to stay then, but you can't, you know."

"Well, when that day comes it'll be because I want to go more than I want to stay."

Acy shut his eyes tightly for a moment. The girl still retained her faculty for cast iron logic and it never failed to amaze him.

She was thoughtful for a while. "You know, I don't think I like the way what I just said sounded."

Acy palmed a half smile. Whatever her flair for abrupt and pointed thinking made her say, she was not without sensitivity. "Why, Sugar?"

"Because it sounded as though I'd stop loving you and appreciating what you've done for me and that's not true … but a girl has to marry sometime, doesn't she?"

"Any gal as fine as you. Don't you worry. If the time ever comes for you to leave, ole Acy'll be damn sorry to see you go, but he wouldn't hold you if he could."

Acy dabbed a trickle of cherry ice cream from his chin and sat back. "That was a holiday, Sugar … now how long have I got to diet to lose what I've gained?"

Cyri concentrated hard for a moment. "I think a week on one toothpick and half a glass of water a day will do the trick."

Acy groaned while Willie, who sat in a corner on his ubiquitous stool, chuckled merrily. "That will be sterile grist for his honor's capacious maw."

Acy frowned at the colored man. "Since when did you pick up this here 'your honor' stuff?"

"A mere dash of spice to an otherwise tasteless salutation … the 'here' was superfluous."

"Cut out superfluity, my man, and you'd have to stay quiet half the time," retorted Acy triumphantly.

Cyri laughed heartily while Willie inclined his head in mock humility. "It is painful to sit and allow one's self to be maligned and not raise a hand to stop it."

"You never do raise a hand," snarled "his honor." "You sure give that tongue hell, though."

Later in the living room, Cyri lay at full length on the bear skin, clad in briefs and a bra, looking at the latest *Life*. Acy sat in his chair and nodded comfortably, allowing his dinner to settle into place before retiring. He watched the flickering firelight play on her skin, dancing and caressing her like clutching passionate fingers. He stirred and sat a little straighter. "Sugar, I think you should have more friends."

She looked up, her even teeth flashing in the firelight. "I'm satisfied."

"I know, but it isn't right. Kids your age should be kicking up their heels and enjoying themselves. If you stay here too long you'll get set in your ways, like me and Willie and Daisy."

"Is that bad?"

Acy sighed. She could be difficult. "You," he accused roughly, "know what I'm talking about."

She smiled again and rolled over on her back, stretching her arms over her head and extending her legs and toes as far as they would go in a delicious stretch. The sight of her pliant body glowing with health made Acy gasp as he did a dozen times a day for one reason or another.

"What do you want me to do," she asked as she sat up, her hair pouring over her shoulder like a cascade of silk.

"It'll be summer in another month," he said. "I want you to go out to the lake and meet people."

"How do you know they'll be the right people?"

"If they aren't you'll know it and let them alone. I'm not afraid of that, Sugar."

Her face grew serious. "Acy, you've forgotten all about what I was before I came to you, haven't you?"

He shrugged. "No, I ain't fergot it. I just disremember it. It's hard to explain, but somehow just because you were the one who did those things takes the sting out of 'em. In a sense you didn't know what you were doing and therefore, how can anyone blame you or hold it against you … in the usual sense that people are blamed? You don't beat a little puppy to death because he pee-pees on the floor. You might rub his nose in it and cure him, but on the other hand, you might ruin him. These things have to have individual solutions. Take you, fer instance. As long as you been here you ain't done a single thing I'd be ashamed of my daughter doin'. You've done what I asked you to do and I never had to tell you twice. What more can a man ask?"

She slid over and rubbed her forehead on his knee, her favorite gesture of affection. Her green eyes, steady, if a little misty, held his for a moment. "There just aren't any more men like you, Acy."

He took two handfuls of her glistening hair and let it fall through his fingers, drinking in the sensation through his sensitive skin. "I'm just a fat man with a soft heart," he murmured as his hands became empty, "but you are a child of the gods, guided by their hands through perils that make me shudder, to my door ... me, out of all the good people on this earth ... you came to me."

"And you let me stay."

He chuckled reminiscently. "If I'da made you go, Willie would have quit me ... him and Daisy, too."

She sighed. "There was a book that said that good things and bad things come in threes."

He grinned. "It's a lie. There ain't but one of you."

Rod Pettingill shook his head to clear away a dizziness that had nothing to do with his libations of the night before. Cyri sat beside him in the pavilion and kicked up the sawdust with her feet, drank her Coke and chatted as companionably as though she had known him all her life. This in itself was unusual. If she was using the ingénue touch as a part of a line, then she was by far the most complete mistress of the art he had ever seen, and Rod had known many women in his life.

He had been a connoisseur of lines and bodies for a long time, and never had any come within even easy reach of Cyri.

Although her proportions were of the very best, she might not have been picked from a crowd of pretty young girls at a hundred feet, but from twenty-five feet on up to zero her quality was instantly apparent. He thought of Mary Jane and immediately put her out of his mind as though to think of them both at the same time was some sort of sacrilege. Being a man of action, he longed to mouth her pink ears and caress her skin with his hands. He wanted to taste her lips, to force them apart and feel the enamel of her white teeth, to burnish the skin under her lips with his tongue.

She smiled, making the skin of his back wriggle like a horse trying to dislodge a fly. "Do you hurt?"

"Yes," he heard himself say and almost failed to recognize his own voice.

She sensed the serious tone and her smile faded. "I'm sorry ... do you hurt, really?"

He could see the melting concern flare immediately in the depths of her eyes and a swift pain started at his sternum and worked its way into his windpipe where it tried to choke him. His laugh was hollow and unconvincing. "No, not really, only ..."

"What, Rod? You can tell me."

"I don't guess I could, Cyri, not ..."

"But, why? Aren't we friends?"

He couldn't duck that one and he was left a little dizzy. He had known her one exciting hour and she now was his friend. The strange thing was the inescapable certainty that she meant what she was saying. Rod, in his associations, was not accustomed to frankness and Cyri had so rocked his aplomb that he had a chilling desire to flee. He had wanted to possess many women and oddly enough, though he wanted to possess Cyri, there was a difference he could not explain. He, who had never before found it necessary to look at himself in askance, now knew that if he

ever possessed her it would be she who wanted it, she who ...
No, it was not conceivable that this wonderful creature would
ever make advances to him. The pain in his throat irritated him,
his utter capitulation irritated him because it initiated a host of
reactions to which he was an utter stranger. Rod had occupied
his position of high man on the pole for so long that any other
position was strange.

"I asked you if we weren't friends," she prompted.

"Why er ... of course, Cyri!" He faced her squarely and met
the power of her eyes without wavering. "May I say that you are
the most wonderful person I ever knew?" He felt like a fool, he
sounded a fool, and clenched his teeth in silent vexation.

She smiled again as a great understanding burst upon her.
Now she knew what was wrong and the knowledge excited her.
"You may say that I'm the most wonderful person in *appear-
ance* you ever knew."

Rod, who was not slow at smart back chat, now flunked dismally by asking, "Why just that?"

"Because you've hardly known me an hour and you're saying
things about me that you couldn't possibly know."

He took the blow like a man, swallowed noisily and nodded.
"Yes, I guess you have me there. Anyhow, that's how I feel now."

"I admit the possibility all right. I feel some things about you
that I may be wrong about, things I can't really know. I didn't
mean to imply that such a reaction was abnormal or anything."

"What is it you know about me?"

She shook her head, but her smile was a note of understanding and forgiveness.

"But," he said, grabbing a handful of her ammunition, "we're
friends, aren't we?"

She nodded and whimsically berated herself for falling into
the trap. She was learning that there was a time for silence and

a time for speech. "Rod, I'm going to say something that might sound odd … you're making me do it. It might sound stuffy and upstage … do you still want me to tell you?"

He nodded vigorously. "More now than ever."

She kicked more sawdust and wriggled her toes, scratching their sensitive inner surfaces with the abrasive. She sighed and lifted her head. "You are in love with me … in just this little while, you are in love with me, or you think you are which amounts to the same thing until you find out differently."

She had done it. She had stripped the last mystery that he could ever have hoped to keep from her and it left him feeling like a flag pole in a cold wind. Was she a witch, was she fey to creep beneath the defenses of a life time and reduce them to nothing? Did he dare think as his mind was accustomed to thinking when with a beautiful woman? A heavy red flush spread slowly over his face and he looked down at the sawdust where her shapely feet had cut twin trenches.

"What else do you know," he asked, his voice hoarse and strained.

"I know that what I said upset you," she told him quietly.

It wasn't too bad, he thought. Anyone could see that. "What else?"

"You don't want me to tell you, Rod. People like those with whom you were reared would probably think that your thoughts weren't nice."

Abruptly, he stood up. "Let's go … How did you come out here?"

She rose with sinuous grace, handling her body with perfect fluid ease. "I came out on the bus."

"I'll take you home."

As they walked across the sand to the bath house, neither spoke a word and when they had dressed and were in his car headed back to town, Cyri said, "Rod, did I make you angry?"

"No, Cyri," he said gently. "You upset me to hell and gone, that's all. I don't understand you, you baffle me, you make me feel small and rotten and insignificant. You know what goes on in the back of my mind and I've spent a lifetime trying to carry a face that was blank to what went on behind it."

"Why?" she asked.

Rod tensed his muscles and hunched his back and strove to keep his thoughts in order.

"Were you ashamed of your thoughts?" she persisted.

The question was almost like a shot of dope to his confusion. "Yes," he said frankly, and felt vastly relieved.

"I'm never ashamed of what I think," she said. "I'm never ashamed of what I do."

"Then you've never done anything," he said confidently.

Cyri leaned back in the car and tossed her hair back in the wind where it flowed about her shoulders. "I don't know how to talk to people like you."

"How do you mean?"

"I'm about to tell you something and I don't think you'll like it."

"Tell me anyway. What do you care whether I like it or not?"

She shrugged. "Well, you say I've never done anything. I let a man, a boy rather, have me when I was very young and many times after that."

Rod felt a chill touch his spine and his thoughts previously incoherent because of their speed became more so because they had doubled back on themselves and produced hopeless chaos.

"And you aren't ashamed of that?"

"No. Should I be?"

"Cyri, you're not a wanton … I don't care what you tell me." His voice had an agonized tautness that seemed to pain him. "I know that. You're good and fine and sweet. You can't be like you say."

"I'm afraid you don't quite understand. I don't any more and when I did I was too young to know any better. I do know better now, but I'm not ashamed of what has happened in the past. Acy says it's a waste of time to worry over what's happened in the past."

"Who's Acy?"

"He's the most wonderful man in the world. He's been a father to me."

"You live with him?"

"Yes. He has a bar on Bourbon Street and we live up stairs."

"Oh, yes. You mean the Old Barrel House."

"Yes, that's it. The happiest days of my life have been spent there."

"Well … Hell, I know him. He weighs over three hundred pounds. He's a legend in the Quarter."

She smiled. "He weighs only two hundred and eighty now. I made him go on a diet. He gripes all the time but he feels better and looks better than he ever did."

They drove for some time in silence which Rod found less endurable than her punishingly blunt conversation.

"Cyri, what do you think of me? Maybe I oughtn't ask that question but I have to."

She turned her steady eyes on him. "I don't know, really. There are some things that stand out like whitewashed posts in the moonlight, but back of them there is a great darkness. I can't see what the darkness holds."

"About those posts … are they nice posts?"

"They're not bad. That word nice … I distrust it. There are too many ways to interpret it and too much personal opinion in the interpretation."

"Well, give me a for instance … besides what you gave me before."

"Well, for one thing, you've been terribly spoiled …"

"Hold it there," he put in. "Why do you say that?"

"Because one of the brightest posts in the moonlight is your, let's call it desire for me and yet you've been a perfect gentleman. You haven't been a perfect gentleman always, Rod, where women are concerned."

"I bow my head to your insight," he said with a wry grin. "May I ask how you arrived at that conclusion?"

"I can't explain it well. I can sense it. A man would hardly have approached me like you did unless he had had considerable experience. He would have been afraid of getting the cold eye. If you had just been spoiled at home, life outside would have taken a lot of it out of you before now. Everyone, including women, have spoiled you. You're very handsome, you present a good appearance, and you probably have been accustomed to getting your own way most of the time."

"I have never seen anyone in all my life quite as wide open as you," he told her with a sort of whimsical vexation. "Don't you ever play it close in order to be mysterious and make people wonder what goes on in your mind?"

"No. I don't like that sort of thing. I think it is a form of dishonesty that is, in a manner, underhanded because there is no defense for it. Either I tell you what I think or you will never know. You may guess and you may speculate, but you never know. If two people expect to get along, how can they if there are all sorts of defenses and secrets? I don't mean that two people need to tell each other everything, that wouldn't work either. I mean things that matter."

Rod chuckled. "Anyhow, this is a new experience and I love it." He swung the car over on a street that was shaded with trees on which was very little traffic. He pulled up in front of a deserted house and stopped.

"If you like frankness, then I'm going to be frank. I've only known you a short while. I'll admit freely that you have upset me as I've never been before. Be that as it may, I want to put my arms around you and I want to kiss you. May I?"

A slow delightful smile crept slowly across her face as she watched him. "You never asked that question before, did you?"

"No, I never asked that question before and if you say no I'll take you home and we'll still be friends."

She studied the clean-cut line of his jaw, the well-tanned skin fitted rather tightly over good facial structure, his full, rather petulant lips and the hazel depths of his long lashed eyes. "I think it would be rather nice."

He drew her tenderly into the crook of his right arm, his heart banging noisily against the wall of his ribs shaking him like the blows of a steam hammer. He touched her face with the left hand and hooked the soft hair back of her ear, trying to avoid the steadiness of her eyes and the half smile on her lips. There was something uncanny about her attitude, objective and without the usual struggle and eventual capitulation. As his lips grew nearer, she closed her eyes and inclined her face to meet him. The touch was of such soft wrenching delight that his head swirled madly and hot blood roared thunderously in his ears. Expertly he wove a pattern over her lips, making full use of much practice and observation, finally being rewarded by the relaxing of her jaws. He drew a whistling breath through his nose and his arms gripped her hard, thrusting her head back against the seat where the advance stab of her tongue sent bursts of agonizing joy through his body. Her own arms became tight about his neck and he felt the new warmth that seemed to sear him from chest to knee as she urged herself against him, soft yet firm, clinging as nature, resenting the interfering textile that separated them, trying to overcome its presence by hard pressure and insistance.

By mutual accord, they sat back letting air again flood their lungs, Rod feeling much like a man who has been living in fear of death and suddenly sees life ahead. A storm of unaccustomed emotion struck him and for the first time in many years forced tears to his eyes. Angrily, he fought them away and blew his nose on a clean white handkerchief. Cyri lay relaxed on the seat, letting her body soak up the delight of his kiss, letting sensations awake in her that had been dormant for a long time. She thought of her talk with Daisy several weeks ago and made a resolution to tell the old woman that she was right.

"I'd better take you home now."

"Why, Rod, didn't you enjoy it?"

"My God … enjoy it? It almost killed me. I've never been really kissed before and now I know it."

"Then it seems you'd want more."

He gripped the steering wheel and strove to think of something to say to her. "I liked it so much and I want so much more that I don't trust myself with you any longer. I'm afraid to. Remember, I'm not trained in resistance."

Her smile made him ache all over. "I'm not either, Rod."

"And you're not afraid?"

"No."

For a full minute, he tried to detect the slightest wavering of her eyes, the slightest coyness or coquetry, but he could see none. Her eyes were as steady as set gems and her gaze did not falter in the least. An overpowering desire to shriek and tear his clothes came over him, to beat his head with his fists to bring some semblance of order. Instead, he started the motor and tore away from the spot, his motor whining reproachfully.

She still sat limply on the seat in a rosy haze, a little sorry that he hadn't kissed her again, because there was something special about it, something for which she hadn't been prepared, something that actually made him look differently now.

"Rod, Willie says it isn't good to race the motor like that."

"Who in hell is Willie?"

"He's a colored man who works for Acy. He speaks wonderful English."

"Holy angels of mercy, protect me for just a little longer," he muttered to himself as he turned into Bourbon Street and raced toward the Old Barrel House. He skidded to a stop in front of the bar and opened the door for her.

"It was nice meeting you, Cyri, it really was."

She stepped out and smiled. "I enjoyed it, Rod. We'll have to do it again sometime."

"Er … yes, by all means." Again the motor strained at the load of gas he thrust upon it and it screeched away from the Old Barrel House.

CHAPTER SIX
—CYRI STEPS OUT

CYRI WALKED in and waved gaily to Acy who quickly dropped his hand in which was an egg he had cajoled from Daisy, exceeding his normal quota by one. "Hiya, gal. Have a good time?"

"Wonderful," she said as she came over to the bar. "I met the most delightful man and he fell in love with me ... at sight."

Acy's mouth dropped open, revealing masticated egg. "He what?"

She nodded gleefully. "Did I ever throw him into a tizzy."

The fat man swallowed his egg and chased it with beer. "Bet y' did too. What was he in such an all-fired hurry to get away for? Could hear his tires screechin' all the way in here."

She grinned impishly. "I think I had him a little confused. He's gone home to think it all over."

Acy grinned back. "I'm sure glad it ain't me that's got to go home and try to figger you out. Git on upstairs. You're out of bounds."

She made a face at him and turning, raced to the stairs.

"Don't look now," whispered Willie, "but your language is terrible this afternoon." Willie escaped the resultant glare by turning and walking away.

A natty man in a loud striped suit, hand painted tie, and lacquered shoes came up to the bar and smiled ingratiatingly at Acy.

"Say, feller, that girl's O.K. How's about breaking me down to her. I'd give a week's pay to date her."

Acy choked back the raw rage that gripped him by the throat like steel fingers and forced himself to be calm. "Y'would hunh?"

"Sure would, pal," said the other. "Slip me the pass word and I'll make it worth your while."

"You wanta get broke down to her ... is that right?"

"That's right, pal. I can be generous to my friends."

"Me too, brother," said Acy bitingly. "I'm gonna break you down ..." His open hand landed atop the man's head with crushing force, smashing him to the floor by sheer power. He leaned over the bar. "Not to her, though, you tight-skinned, shiny fingered, slick pantied, tallow-headed, rope-gutted son of a bitch ... *Willie!* Throw this here goddamn load of fertilizer into the street and I mean *throw* him."

Amid snickers from the customers, Willie picked the slight man up by the trousers seat and dumped him vigorously into the street.

Acy fumed mightily. "Hummmmpap ... stuppft ... Burruf ... goddamn irritation, stinkin', blinkin' imposition, that's what ... crumby bastard. Fish-gutted, snakeeyed, son of a slit tongued Mongolian whore. Pooffffurt."

"Restrain your righteous anger," advised Willie. "Ignoble gentleman quite well repaid for his temerity."

Acy wriggled, still smouldering with rage. "Bat-eared, camel backed, baboon-faced son of an aborted elephant."

"Recall," persisted Willie, "that eminent physician advised greatly against such outbursts. Made cogent reflections on state of your honor's arteries."

"T'hell with the doctor and you too," snarled Acy. "What d'ye want me to do, sit here and bust wide open?"

A gale of laughter swept the customers and for a few moments the cash register rang unceasingly as everyone took the occurrence as an excuse to refill.

Mrs. Pettingill swept into the library like an inefficient model of some ancient aircraft attempting to take off. She was dressed in yards of lavender chiffon with innumerable flounces, ruffles and other tripperies that seemed to add to her rather notable avoirdupois. She had the shelved front and protuberant rear of the female who has outgrown the effectiveness of any sort of boned restraint, no matter how well or strongly made, but has not stopped trying.

"Rodney," she cooed chidingly. "I've called you twice for dinner. It's getting cold."

"I don't want any dinner."

"But sitting here in the dark like this ... alone. Are you ill?"

"No, mother, I'm not ill. Now please go away and ... no, sit down a moment, will you? I want to ask you a few questions."

She gave him a penetrating glance. "Certainly, son. What's bothering you?"

He lit a cigarette before replying. "Mother, what sort of people are we?"

Mrs. Pettingill swallowed jerkily. "Well ... to tell you the truth, I don't know what you're talking about."

"Are we good people, middle class, or scum?"

"Why, Rodney, what a thing to ask. We are, of course, the very best of people. Your two uncles on your father's side are United States senators. One, Uncle Charles, was even talked about for Vice President, last election. On my side, my grandfather was mayor of Baton Rouge and his father before him was a general in the Army. Our ancestry goes back to the first Earl of...."

"Oh, come, mother, haven't we any better reason for shouting than men who are dead or those who managed to acquire a cornfield, slop-tongued dialect which is a Southern politician's sharpest weapon?"

Cornelia Pettingill gasped for breath and peered at her son as though he was about to run amuck. "Are you quite sure you're well?"

"I'm well and you answered my question in just the manner I expected you to. In other words, you have said exactly nothing."

"Rodney!" She was manifestly shocked.

"It's true. You repeated the selfsame things that all our crowd repeats if the manner of breeding comes up. Hasn't anyone in this family ever *done* anything?"

"Well ... whatever outrageous thing you now have in mind, I might point out that your father is an eminently respected stock broker and a very successful one, and I have been called a model mother."

Rod sighed. "Yes, I suppose you're right."

"Of course I'm right. Rodney, whatever put this sort of thing into your head?"

"A girl, mother."

"A girl ... what girl?"

"Oh, one I met at the beach to-day. She apparently is a nobody and yet she could walk down St. Charles, take any single man away from his girl and make half the married ones leave home."

"Oh, pshaw. What a ridiculous thing to say. I dare say she may be pretty in a cheap sort of way, like they are sometimes, but the trouble with that sort is they could never match your culture and intelligence. That's the trouble with women like that, son. They have looks and no brains, to say nothing of background or any real touch with the right things and people."

"The right things and the right people," he muttered half to himself. "I'd like to say, mother, that the dumb thing put me in such a tailspin in about half an hour that I haven't recovered from it yet; and yet, she, out of all the women I ever met, started me wondering whether all these things are as good as they've been preached."

By this time, Mrs. Pettingill realized completely, if tardily, that whoever this girl was, with whatever background, she had most certainly delivered a mortal blow to the heart of her son. It was not and had never been her intention that this only offspring, this apple of her eye, this expensive and in many ways disappointing bit of posterity, should marry beneath what she considered his station. Just what this station was one might imagine by considering that peculiar state of myopia induced by the advent of a single manchild, in the case of the mother. No female yet conceived was half good enough for him, she had told herself repeatedly; this little dint of thaumaturgical logic being arrived at by the same obscure chemistry which produced the eye condition. There were women whom she would have suffered as his wife, candidates from a very select strata, candidates who would of course be, at best, only tolerated substitutes for that state of perfection which is never reached, but which she was convinced permeated her son from the hour of his birth.

In one burst of icy, flaring brightness, Cornelia Pettingill saw that at long last had come the war, and she did not intend to open battle without weapons. "Rodney, it appears that you are serious."

His smile was what one might expect in an attempt to be brave after a broken leg. "Comes as a shock, doesn't it. Well, me too. It's like having worn shoes all one's life, then find it necessary to run a race barefooted over washed gravel. The knives I'm accustomed to, enter without pain and leave no scars. These new ones, ones I've never known about before to-day, must have been dipped in *curare*."

"Let's eat dinner now, son, and afterward we'll talk about her. I may be entirely wrong about her. She may be the perfect girl."

Rodney leaped to his feet and kissed his mother resoundingly. "Now I believe I could eat. Lead me to it."

Rodney's father, although a man reared in the same tradition as his son, had discovered early in his youth that he had been taken on many points. Now that he was greyed, a little bent, but still full of a notable fire, he had drifted by easy stages into an entirely self contained and totally concealed cynicism which is by far the worst sort of cynicism. In his home and among his acquaintances, he had acquired the reputation of being a pillar of stability, a man of impeccable tastes, dependable, securely attached to his household and in many ways a perfect husband. Using this formidable bulwark of respectability, he had found it comparatively easy to visit Miss Amanda Pennyworth in the apartment for which he had been paying some eleven years.

That Miss Pennyworth had a cake of Mississippi sod for a mind was a welcome relief from those of his own circle who lived under the delusion that their own craniums were occupied by brains. They weren't, of course, but the delusion is widespread in certain strata, seeming in some obscure way to be related to the classic symbol for success and intelligence, the dollar mark. The emanations of Amanda's fundamental but soothing bit of sod were to Gerald Pettingill's genteel irritations what a cold drink of water would be to a worker suddenly forced on a diet of tasty, but unsatisfying, champagne. She chattered, but she did not demand that he listen, which was a change and a vigorous relief.

She exposed, upon demand, a tremendous expanse of tender, smooth white skin and her billowing wealth of blonde hair had a delightful habit of tickling his nose and making him sneeze.

There was so much of it that it tickled him in many places at the same time, lending a touch of piquancy to what is otherwise somewhat limited as regards surprise, novelty, and piquancy ... especially after eleven years. She was pretty, she was as friendly as a spaniel, as unprincipled as a mongrel pussy searching for adventure on a back fence, and never bored Gerald with things that might be unpleasant. Amanda, in her own way, made better use of her sod than many of Gerald's acquaintances had their alleged brains because she never tried to exceed its limitations.

"Rodney," said Cornelia as she pounded into the dining room, "is in love."

The bombshell left Gerald singularly chill. He looked up from his soup in a perfunctory manner and grunted non-committally. Harking back to certain experiences in the past, he hastily amended the grunt. "That's fine ... perfect."

Cornelia drove the poised cloud from her brow and smiled at her son with as little sincerity as had marked her husband's remark.

"We think she is a really fine girl," added Cornelia.

"Ummm hummm. Oh, certainly ... indeed so. Anything like Mary Jane?"

"Indeed not," retorted Cornelia, bridling. She had never forgiven Mary Jane for marrying that rich foreigner when she might have had Rodney. "Mary Jane behaved abominably ... after all we did for her, accepting her as our equal ... her and her family."

Rodney ate his soup silently and let his parents do the talking. He had always been a little in awe of his father because he had long entertained a suspicion that the old man concealed a great deal behind that bland countenance. That remark about Mary Jane, for instance. What, actually, had he known of their relationship? Much or nothing? One could not say, simply because that was the way Gerald wanted it. Then, too, there had been the time on Carondelet Street when Rod had seen whom he was certain could have been no one but his father, but there had been a lush blonde cuddled in the crook of the man's arms. This should not have been Gerald, but was it? If so, Rod betrayed his mother by achieving a new and deeper respect for his father. The old man had deserved something for himself other than a life of respectable ennui and though Rod would not be certain, he began to suspect that he had actually seen his father on his way to fun and frolic.

"Rod," continued Cornelia, "is going to ask her to dinner as soon as he can so we can see her."

Gerald wondered if Rodney knew his mother well enough to realize what this apparent acquiescent attitude portended, giving his son a quick, searching glance. Rod did not intercept the glance but felt it, feeling also another twinge of kinship with his father. So he knew, too. Well, he'd give it a try. First, because he was anxious for parental approval; second, because he had a faintly sadistic desire to see what would happen when the two women got together. Cyri, whose forthrightness was as blunt and forceful as a sledge, and Cornelia, who had been schooled in gesture, falsehood, and devious speech and thought. It would not take long for his mother to get rocked to the nethermost reaches of her false teeth and this he had to see whatever the cost.

Acy slid his schooner toward Willie and hissed *sotto voce,* "Gimme another fill there, Willie."

Willie was whipping a Sazarac into being and paid no attention, affecting not to have heard.

"Psssttt," hissed Acy, shaking the mug suggestively, keeping his eye on the first landing of the stairs. Willie went on with his mixing, blandly ignoring his employer. "Willie," grated Acy without moving his lips, "if you don't turn your hot damned head and gimme some o' that there lager …"

" 'That there' is very poor grammar," murmured Willie, pouring the drink into a thick glass.

"Hah, knew that'd bring you to life, now …"

Acy hastily slid the mug under the bar and turned his attention to the lithograph of Custer being scalped by the Indians that he had been threatening to burn for ten years. It was fly specked and hideous, but it had been there so long that though he hated it, he let it hang. Now he studied it with great concentration. He could feel the closeness of the girl at his elbow, but he continued to study the picture. Finally he turned.

"Well, if it ain't my Sugar … how you feeling, Sugar?" He laughed, but it sounded like the ring of a phony coin.

"What were you grinding your teeth at Willie for," she asked, ignoring his spurious effusiveness.

"Oh … er, Willie? Well, he's been sorta slow tonight. Needs spurring a little every now and then … got to keep 'im on the ball … slowed up lately … old, probably. Yeah … Gettin' …"

"I don't believe a word of it," she interrupted his failing defense. "I think you were trying to wheedle more beer out of him."

"Who, me?" Acy's surprise was painted on his face like the make-up of a street walker.

She turned to Willie. "Am I right, Willie?"

"It would not be sportsmanlike to inform on respected employer."

"I thought so. What would you say if I told you that you could have only three crackers and a small green salad for dinner?"

Acy looked lugubrious. "But, Sugar, I been working all day and I need food."

"You'll get food in the right quantities and at the right times. If I catch you fudging again, I'll put you on bread and water. There haven't been any phone calls for me?"

"If there was, I'da buzzed you. Ain't been none."

"Any," corrected Willie as he placed money before the fat man.

"There have been no phone calls," said Acy in a carefully precise falsetto, glaring at Willie.

At that moment, the phone rang and Willie answered it. He turned and gestured toward Cyri with the receiver. "For the Princess."

"Thanks, Willie." She took the receiver from him and said, "Hello."

"Hello, Cyri, this is Rod."

"Yes?"

Rod drew his breath sharply. Her tone was definitely short. "Well, I thought I'd call and see how you were doing."

"I'm doing fine."

"That's good … I'm glad to hear it."

"What did you really call for, Rod?"

He gripped the phone a little tighter, passively aware that his palms were sweating. "Well, to tell you the truth, Cyri, mother wants to see you."

"Didn't you give her my address?"

A blob of sweat detached itself from his forehead and ran into his eye. "Cyri, my mother can't go into a bar."

"Why?"

"It isn't … Will you come to dinner tomorrow night? I've talked a lot about you and … you know how mothers are."

"No, I'm afraid I don't. How are they?"

Rod made a sound that sounded somewhat like a bleat of despair. "Cyri, it isn't at all unusual for a man to invite a girl to his house for dinner. Will you come?"

"Certainly. What shall I wear?"

Rod lowered his voice. "I think she's intending to catch you unawares because I heard her tell Pop that he'd have to dress for dinner when you came, so you'd better wear an evening dress. The prettiest you have. I want you to knock 'em dead at first sight."

"You mean she'd do that and not let me know?"

"She would, but I can't explain that now. It's just the way some women are ... mothers, sometimes."

"What time shall I arrive?"

"Oh, I'll come by and pick you up. We'll cut a figure, Cyri. I'll borrow Dad's Cadillac."

"Cadillacs aren't so hot," she told him informatively. "Acy's got a Jaguar that'll do one hundred and thirty miles an hour."

"He has.... oh ... that's fine. I'll pick you up at seven and we'll have time to meet the family before dinner. O.K. with you?"

"Yes, I'll be ready." She dropped the receiver on the cradle and turned around, her brow thoughtful. Acy's voice interrupted her study.

"Since when has my Ford turned into a Jaguar?"

She smiled wickedly. "He was bragging, so I thought I'd bring him down a peg or two. Acy, I don't have a dinner dress."

"Go git one."

"But they cost a lot of money and I just don't like the idea of dressing up to suit his stinky old mother. He says she is going to dress them all up and wasn't going to tell me about it so as to make me look tacky. I don't think I'm going to like her."

"She must be a blasted fool," roared Acy, turning red. "Who the hell she think she is anyhow?"

"That's what I want to know. Now I *really* want to knock her damn eyes out."

Acy slapped the bar. "I'll do the cussin' round here. Ladies don't cuss." Several men at the bar laughed aloud and the fat man's face flamed again.

Cyri laughed with them. "I just did it to show you how it sounded. I wonder where I can get the cutest dinner dress in town … better ask Daisy, I guess."

"Daisy is doubtless in possession of desired information, Princess," put in Willie. "That female has a way of knowing everything."

"You mean like the time you took that bubble dancer on the Zulu Parade at Mardi Gras?"

Willie's protective coloring prevented visible flushing, but he followed out the rest of it to perfection. "Princess, it is better to allow the incident go unreminded. Daisy can become most abusive when she thinks of it, which is too often."

Acy didn't know where the evening dress came from, nor did he care. He only knew that on Cyri it took on something that few women ever manage to lend clothing. It was a simple sheath-like thing that fit with heart-stopping perfection. It was a rich ivory white with deep pleats running from waist to hem, the inside of the pleats faced with green that peeped only when she walked. Her hair was parted and swept back, massing on her shoulders where it slid back and forth with the slightest motion of her head. Acy sat and watched her pirouette before the mirror, feeling the sting of tears in his eyes. He wiped them away and sighed. Then getting laboriously to his feet, he walked to a wall safe and withdrew a rusted old box. He opened it and brought out two heavy silver bracelets set with exquisitely carved jade so nearly matching her eyes that he looked at the baubles as though seeing them for the first time. There was also a choker necklace to match. He took them to her and said, "Sugar, I once swore that no woman would ever wear these again. I was a fool and I want you to wear them."

She gasped as she took the necklace from his hands. "Oh, Acy, what gorgeous things. They must have cost a fortune and they just match my dress."

"And your eyes," he added.

She smiled wistfully. "Acy, I want to wear them, but please don't let me if it hurts you. They must have belonged to her." She nodded toward the portrait over the mantel.

He nodded. "That's right, and I think if she were here she would have had them on you before now."

She kissed him with gentle sweetness. "I love you, Acy. You'll never know how much."

"I will too," he said smiling, "because I know something of your capacity."

She put on the necklace which gleamed dully with a rich somnolent fire against the marble smoothness of her breast and neck.

Acy muttered to himself. "Silver, ivory and jade adorning a soul brighter than any, more precious than all."

He was downstairs sitting before the cash register when Rodney Pettingill came in.

"I beg your pardon, sir. I didn't know any other entrance."

"All right, son. I'll buzz her. Gerald Pettingill's son, eh?" He touched a button beneath the bar.

"Yes, sir. I've been in here before. A year or so ago."

"Got pretty drunk, didn't you?"

Rod flushed and wriggled his neck around in his stiff evening collar. "I'm afraid I did, sir."

"Come over here, son. I want to tell you something." Rod walked closer. "I ain't telling the girl who she can go with and who she can't. I ain't said a word about you to her, but I know plenty. I know about the apartment you paid for for a long time. I know you been run outa some good schools. In other words, you ain't no bargain, don't make no difference how you look at it. You live off your pa and so far you ain't turned a hand to earn an honest dollar."

Rod opened his mouth to speak, but Acy raised his hand. "Hear me out and I don't aim to say another word when I'm done. As I say, I ain't tellin' her who she can go with and who she can't. There's just one thing I want you to remember. That gal is a fine hunk o' woman. You so much as put a scratch on her and there ain't enough gold in Fort Knox to keep me from wringing you out like a wet dishrag. I don't like to threaten, but I think if you know the facts right off you'll have no comeback if I ever have to work out on you."

Rod attempted to shrug away the ants that had established a runway up and down his spine. He did manage to hold the gaze of those flinty yellow eyes, although the effort cost him greatly. Anger thundered deep inside him but something kept it deep. He was, however, not without courage.

"Then it is your opinion that there's no good in me?"

"I ain't got the faintest idea what's in you. All I say is that none of it ever escaped. By that token there should be plenty left. I'd say it was time you let a little out."

A rueful smile tugged at Rod's lips. "You're frank. I'll say that for you."

"You seem to have a little sense," retorted Acy. "I'll give you that. You didn't foam up and lose your temper like I expected."

"That's called Russian roulette with all the chambers loaded. This is your place. When you speak here, I have to listen."

"Good sense, son. Good sense. Here she comes."

Cyri came down the steps holding her skirt up somewhat with her fingertips, a picture of heartbreaking loveliness from the silky smooth crown of her head to the points of her expensively shod feet. A rustle and several vocal sounds went up from the men in the bar, and one old man who had not missed a day in the Barrel House in fifteen years, started clapping vociferously and Cyri reaped a hail of applause from the patrons. Acy almost burst with pride. Rod steadied himself against the bar and drank deeply of the sight. He, too, felt a wave of pride from the honest applause of these men who ordinarily he would have looked down on.

She thanked them with a graceful nod and smile and marched straight to Rod. "I'm ready."

Rod gulped like a dog trying to swallow a bone and took her arm.

"Wait, I haven't kissed Acy goodbye." She leaned across the bar and kissed him resoundingly. "I'll be in before you go to bed, Acy."

"You better be," he snarled with an attempt at bad humor, "or I'll have the skin off ye."

Gerald Pettingill expected a girl out of the ordinary. He even expected a beautiful girl, but Cyri he did not expect, and the sight of her standing in the living room door with Rod halted him half-way to his feet. He broke a life-long rule and stared, the only thing that prevented him from staring longer was that the girl's eyes were on his and the impact was sufficient to wake him.

"I beg your pardon," he stammered. "My eyes ... you know ... not very good these days." He had been reading the paper without glasses but he did not seem to remember the fact.

They walked in, Cyri leading. She held out her hand which Gerald took, impressed by its strength.

"This is a pleasure, my dear ... it really is." There could be no mistaking the genuine ring of his voice and Rod glanced swiftly, questioningly at his father to see that he was smiling broadly, rather fatuously.

Rod grinned inwardly and asked, "Where's mother?"

"She'll be along in a minute ... here, my dear, take this chair, it is quite comfortable. Er ... will you have a cocktail, or some sherry?"

"Do you have a Martini?"

"Ha ... do I? I make the best Martinis in New Orleans." Gerald bustled over to the little walnut bar and began manufacturing Martinis. Obviously, he was more than pleased with himself. "It is a pleasure to find someone who really appreciates a good Martini. Most of the younger crowd like highballs ... sweet, shudders."

"May I ... I mean, if you have an onion, could I have an onion instead of an olive, please?"

Gerald laughed brightly causing Rod to wriggle in his seat. Never had he heard such an outright explosive laugh from his father. Gerald's laughs were usually well-bred chuckles that could be turned on like a light.

"I know three people who prefer onions," he said. "In all cases they are people of taste and discernment. My onions are special. I make them myself and add a sprig of dill to the brine."

"Why," exclaimed Cyri, "Acy loves dilled onions. He says it gives them a lift."

"Quite... quite," agreed Gerald, pouring out the drinks. "Who is Acy?"

"Her father," put in Rod, hastily.

"Foster father," amended Cyri. "The best man in the world."

Again came that free buoyant laugh as Gerald handed her a Martini. "Not too cold, not put to sleep with ice," he chortled. "As dry as a desert breeze ... wakes up your stomach."

"Mine won't need waking. I'm starved." She tasted her drink and allowed the sparkle of appreciation it brought to her eyes to bathe Gerald. He took a deep breath and sat down feeling that he had slain a dragon.

"This is really superb," said Cyri. "Rod, aren't you drinking?"

"I think I'll try one," said Rod, rising and pouring himself a cocktail.

Gerald winked at her. "Doesn't know the difference between a good Martini and creosote dip."

She laughed at this, the silvery music of her voice sounding a little too robust to be called a tinkle. It was more of a *laugh*. Rod joined hollowly, wondering what they found so funny about it. He had to keep part of his mind on the fact that his mother was delivering a deliberate snub by being late, but he was comforted somewhat by the obvious fact Cyri wasn't conscious of it. What a meeting this would be....

"Ooooh helloooo, there, *everyone*," Cornelia swept grandly into the room, clad in a flowing white chiffon, exuding expensive perfume and a spurious heartiness. She ploughed forward and seized one of Cyri's hands in both of hers. "My *dear*, you don't know how *charmed* I am to meet you. Rod has told *so* much about you. I'm *so* glad you could come and have dinner with us." All of a sudden, the girl's beauty struck her with full force. She halted in mid air, so to speak, strove mightily to regain her composure as though some one had slipped her a straight shot of liquid quinine. She made it and turned to Gerald. "Please, Gerald, might I have one of your inimitable Martinis. I ..." She turned to Cyri again and brutalized her face into a cordial smile. "I didn't expect to see such a perfectly *lovely* young lady, Rod. You should have prepared me ... my dear, you have no *idea* how it is living here with two men. They tell me *nothing*, absolutely nothing. Sometimes I feel that I shall go *mad* ..." She seized the cocktail from Gerald.

"But I thought you said Rod had told you so much about me?"

Rod looked at the ceiling, gripping the cocktail glass with enough force to break it, managing in the process to steal a glance at his father who had stopped in the act of lighting a cigar.

Cornelia swelled, purpled somewhat, then got control again. "Well, I ..." She tried to blast Cyri with a glance and found that the green eyes were much too calm and steady for her. She laughed tinnily. "So he did, but you know how men run on ... they say nothing *really,* they just *enthuse.*" She drank her cocktail at a gulp, forgetting the olive and toothpick, getting the latter caught crossways in her mouth, having to fish for it ignominiously with a forefinger. She flushed and palmed the toothpick. "That, Gerald," she said with well bred malice, "might have choked me."

Cyri smiled at her. "You're supposed to pick the olive up with the toothpick, Mrs. Pettingill ... like this." She picked one up between two slender fingers.

Gerald was seized with a fit of coughing and Rod's forehead dripped with sweat from his tremendous effort to keep back a laugh.

"Indeed," said Cornelia and this time her tones were definitely frigid. "I shall make it a point."

"Do," said Cyri in a friendly manner, still smiling. "Next time it might choke you sure enough."

Maxwell could not have chosen a better time to announce dinner and by the time the soup was disposed of, Cornelia was in a more charitable, therefore more dangerous, frame of mind. The girl's bearing and manners had been impeccable so there was nothing to attack there. She chose another tack.

"My dear, tell us something of your family ... where you came from and the like. You see, we want to know all about you."

That, thought Rod with sinking heart, is no less than the truth.

"I'm afraid my parents weren't very noble people," said Cyri easily. "They both died violent deaths while drunk."

A dreadful silence descended upon the dinner table which Gerald broke in a firm voice. "That is one thing we cannot be blamed for. We neither choose our parents nor can we be blamed for their acts. It is reliably reported that my great grandfather was a horse thief and cattle rustler of considerable strategy and success."

The girl's smile of gratitude made him feel better than buying fifty thousand dollars worth of war bonds.

"Of course, of course," agreed Cornelia hollowly. "One never knows what one will do while under the influence." She seemed to have lost her appetite.

Cyri, on the other hand, seemed intent on her roast and creamed potatoes. She swallowed and faced Cornelia calmly. "In the case of my mother, she heard father say that whiskey didn't grow on trees so she went out to see. I suppose she became angry when he was proved right because she either jumped or fell out of the tree. She broke her neck."

Cornelia turned a little green. "Oh … my … how horrible."

Cyri shrugged. "I think she's better off. She didn't have much happiness."

Making a tremendous effort to steer the conversation into safer channels, Cornelia, whose momentum was carrying her, asked, "Tell us about your present home. Is it uptown?"

Rod's shoulder muscles, already aching from the tension, tightened anew.

"No, I live on Bourbon Street."

"How nice. It is so lovely in the Vieux Carré. Those lovely studio apartments …"

"I live over a bar. It's a pretty big building and Acy owns all of it."

"Over a *bar*. Child, you don't mean it, not *really?*" said Cornelia aghast.

"Certainly I mean it. What's wrong with living over a bar? The happiest years of my life have been spent there."

"Well ... I suppose if *that's* the way you feel about it there's nothing wrong with it." Cornelia was desperately offended.

Gerald wiped his mouth and said, "Better probably than that shack we lived in at Gramercy years ago when I was a twelve dollar a week clerk in the sugar mill."

Cornelia turned pale and sat back in her chair. "I think I'll have to leave the table, Gerald ... all of you ... something has disagreed with me ... I really feel quite faint ..."

Cyri leaped to her feet. "You men go ahead. I'll take Mrs. Pettingill to her room and look after her."

The older woman started, so rapidly did her strength return. "No ... no ... of course not. The idea ... no indeed. I'm not that badly done in, thank you. I'll be *quite* all right ... quite." As she spoke she backed away hurriedly from Cyri and disappeared through an obliging doorway.

"For someone who feels faint, she has quite a lot of scamper, doesn't she?" observed Cyri sitting again in her chair.

Rod bent his head over and rested it on the table, relieving himself of a super load of laughter as quietly as he could, while Gerald covered his purple face with his napkin, his shoulders shaking rapidly.

"My dear ..." He coughed. "You are quite the most priceless person it has ever been my privilege to meet. I would not have taken a million bucks for this."

"I'm afraid I don't understand, sir," admitted Cyri, a perplexed frown on her face.

Gerald stood up and walking around to her chair, planted a kiss on her cheek. "That's to seal a promise I'm about to make. I can see how people brought up outside some of the affectations of society might not understand how the thing worked. It's people like you who have a certain fearful frankness that make people like us squirm. There's nothing wrong with Cornelia. She simply couldn't face the conversation. She'll be all right. I promise you that some day I shall sit down and explain the whole thing in full."

"I guess I'm a little dumb," she said. "You see, I'm only nineteen and I've never been around much or associated with a lot of people. I hope I didn't say anything wrong."

Rod wiped his eyes with a napkin. "What you said was so right that it had atomic results. People are not accustomed to being around so much rightness. It's upsetting ... like you upset me the other day at the beach."

Riding home that night, Rod and Cyri were quiet for a long time. Finally, the girl spoke. "I like your father a great deal, Rod. I don't like your mother at all. As in your case, I see a great many glaring white poles with the dark background, although she is a lot easier to read than you. She came into the living room all prepared to dislike me and yet she went through an elaborate pretense. She thinks you're the world's best and nothing but the best is good enough for you. I'm definitely not it."

"I've been meaning to apologize for her," he said contritely, "but I couldn't think of the right words. I'm really sorry."

"I know you are and so was your father. That still doesn't change her attitude toward me. The reason I'm saying this is because I don't think I'll see you again."

A sudden terrible pain caught Rod by the throat. "Cyri, you can't mean that!"

"I'm thinking ahead, Rod. Apparently, you're not."

"What do you mean?"

"It is not outside possibility that I could fall in love with you. If I did, then the next thing would be marriage. After that would come a terrific row with your family and since you don't have a job, what would we do?"

He hadn't, as a matter of fact, thought as far as marriage, consequently he hadn't thought of the effect it might have on the family. He could be sure of his father's support … he thought, but he could not predict how much effect Cornelia might have on what Gerald would do. For the first time in his life the thought of labor rose in his mind. She was, of course, right, only … why did there have to be a marriage? That was it. Why marry? He thought of the cold eyes of Acy fastened on him, telling him what would happen if anything happened to Cyri. If he could have her just once and overcome her scruples, make her love him so that she'd want him marriage or no marriage, then he'd have things his way. If he could put her up in an apartment as he had Mary Jane, then that would solve everything. He relaxed a little in the seat and swung the car down Canal Street.

"Will you give me some time before you make up your mind, Cyri? There are a few things I want to try to settle at home. Will you wait?"

"Yes, Rod. I'll wait."

"That's my girl. We'll be able to work out something, I'm sure. I couldn't stand the idea of losing you."

"I wouldn't like to lose you, Rod, because I like you an awful lot."

He turned into the French Quarter and finding a dark driveway pulled in and stopped the car.

"I want to kiss you again."

"I want to kiss you, too."

When they finally drew apart, they were weak and shaking and in the dim light from a reflection, he could see her lovely lips half parted, her red tongue trembling from its recent endeavors. With an anguished little cry she came back into his arms and, as if by accident, his hand fell on one scantily covered breast. She flinched and writhed slightly under his touch but she didn't remove his hand. Instead she covered it with her own and pressed it hard against the firm erect mound. The bones of her strapless gown gave to his eager advances and the shock of finding no brassiere almost numbed his hand as it felt the warmth of hot, live flesh. She couldn't keep still in his arms, and the pressure of her own was beginning to hurt his neck and back. He disengaged his mouth and directed its activities elsewhere. A little wail trickled from between her set teeth like water seeping from a dam.

"Please don't put your hands there, Rod … Please …"

"Please, Rod.…" Her knees came together hard. "I can't stop you … please, I can't stand it. I can't … I can't …" With a shuddering moan, she relaxed, sliding forward. She started like a frightened animal and almost instantly there was a bursting flare of raw ecstatic sensation that poured over her body, wrenching her muscles into corded knots and drawing a cry from her lips. She relaxed against him, her hair spilling across his shirt front, her hands slipping from that death grip on the soft flesh under his arms. Then he realized that he had been suffering excruciating pain, but he had not been aware of it.

Never in all his life had he been so thoroughly shaken. It had happened to him, too, and the fact made him angry. Didn't do that when I was a grammar school boy, he accused himself silently. The girl was weeping softly now against his shirt front. At this moment he loved her so much that he grew ill at the thought of what he had done.

Her sobs quieted but she didn't move to cover one thigh that glowed softly in the light that reached them from distant street lamps and the stars. Around them was a canopy of untended banana trees strangely resembling the cracked concrete of the old unused driveway he had chosen. The house looked untenanted with several unglazed windows staring blindly out at the night.

"Cyri ..."

"Yes ... Rod ..." Her arms tightened about him and like a slowly moving white snake her bared leg moved to possess him. His hand reached down and touched the petal smoothness, feeling the leap of fine musculature that reacted to the touch. Her lips sought and found his, and again the hand moved upward, her mouth seeming ravening, yet soft, sweet, yet hard in its hunger. The skin tight barrier of elastic halted his hand momentarily, then gave to his efforts, lighting a fire with her that threatened to consume them both.

She drew her head back and her mouth rippled crookedly as she strove to force speech to her stunned tongue. "Rod ... please, not ... just that again ... can't we ...?" With a hard shudder she collapsed against him, forcing him to hold her. Shock after shock of blistering rapture rocketed up his arms as his hands dug gluttonously into her soft flesh bringing writhings and incoherent pleas.

"Cyri, let's get on the back seat ..."

"Yes ... yes ... yes ..." with frantic haste she squirmed about and skidded out of the door and into the one he opened for her. His arms went about her from behind and his weight bore her to the seat face down. His hands filled with the pure joy of her.

She could feel the chill of the air that struck her and a sensation that made her ears ring with the gathering force of it.

Beginning slowly, it gathered depth and richness, and sent rippling undulations of response through her. Faster, faster … She turned sinuously and took his mouth in hers, straining to kiss him, her cries smothered by his lips. Closer … closer, and then the might of nature smashed them into semi-consciousness leaving dim, puffy echoes of a mighty chorus of concord, dwindling … dwindling into the distance.

"Can you ever forgive me, Cyri … I'm awfully sorry."

She looked up and smiled through her tears. "I'm not sorry, Rod. I was just a little overcome. When I get that way I cry sometimes. It wasn't because of what you did."

"I'll take you home now," he said, his heart singing exultantly. Just one more opportunity of the right sort and she'd be eating out of his hand. Of that he was certain. She hadn't resisted him either time and even the first time she had told him that she wasn't afraid of what might happen.

His conscience, riding the crest of a love he had never felt before, began to prick him. He shouldn't do this to her … unless he was willing to marry her, and that would certainly precipitate a storm at home. This he did not care to experience. His mother was his weapon to use when he needed money and material things, but he knew her ambitions for him and he also knew what ambition did to women like Cornelia. No, it would be much easier to put the apartment to use again. The rent had been paid for three months in advance and only one month had elapsed, so it was still his and he intended to use it.

He backed out into the street and drove rapidly to Bourbon Street and turning into it, pulled up in front of the Old Barrel House. He escorted her to the door of the bar where she turned and faced him.

"Good night, Rod. I won't say I enjoyed it all, but I enjoyed part of it."

He gulped and nodded. "I know, honey. I'll call you as soon as I can find out something."

She leaned forward and kissed him with such impulsive sweetness that he reeled from the impact of it. His ears rang as he opened the car door and sat down.

The bar was filled with patrons, so Cyri waved at Acy and ran lightly up the stairs to her room where she hurriedly slipped from her clothes and fell across the bed. The fine muscles of her stomach contracted as she seemed to feel the mounting progress of the hand that had driven her almost mad with desire. Daisy was right on another count. If you love a person, it makes all sorts of difference.... She sat up and caught her breath. Was she in love with Rod? She turned with the flexibility of a snake and lay on her back, her hair spread out in a dusky fan on the white of the bedspread. It was a question she couldn't answer as yet and even when in the white heat of passion or the cherry red of its sensual aftermath, she did not lose her objectivity.

What if she did love him and he should turn out to be something she couldn't stand? Then she would have to put him out of her life. That she might fail to do this never entered her mind and she felt comforted by the decision.

Curled on the bed, a lithe, pink tan with the tender bloom of exuberant health, she went to sleep, her hands half closed, palms up, lips parted. Two hours later, Acy found her there, breathing with the clocklike respiration of slumber. He sighed and drew the spread over her, awaking her as he did.

She sat up, yawning and rubbing her eyes. "Oh ... hello, Acy."

"I didn't mean to wake you, Sugar. I was just throwing a cover over you."

She smiled with an odd quirk to her lips. "I guess I must have made a picture lying here."

He nodded in dead seriousness. "A picture many an artist has broken his arm to paint and never made it."

Her smile was so sleepily sweet that Acy's big heart ached. "Do you suppose," she asked, frowning a little, "that after all, I'm wrong and other people are right?"

"I'd say that it was most unlikely … knowing you and knowing people."

"That's bias speaking now, Acy. I mean really."

He sat on the edge of the bed and ran a hand lightly over her satiny shoulder. "Suppose you tell me what you mean exactly."

"Well, tonight, for instance. I was out with people who get along very well with society, people who have money and who know what to do under given circumstances. I was the odd ingredient. I was the one who so thoroughly upset Mrs. Pettingill that she went to bed. I was the one who made Rod and his father laugh till they almost fell over. I think they were laughing at her, but they could have been laughing at me. Anyway you look at it, I was the off note. Another girl would have gone there and done the right things, fawned properly on Mrs. Pettingill and all would have been well."

"What about Mr. Pettingill?" asked Acy.

"He's a dear, and I think he liked me a lot."

"Very well, evidently he didn't think you were such an odd ingredient."

She nodded slowly. "Maybe, but I thought possibly he liked me because I was something of a novelty, like Rod when we first met. He was in ants the whole time he was with me that day. Even after tonight, he's still ill at ease and looks like he's waiting for me to break a plate glass window or something."

"What," asked Acy, "is this power you have to upset people?"

She smiled, reminiscently. "You ought to know. I upset you enough times."

"Still that, huh?"

"I suppose so ... it must be, but I can't see why people can't stand being talked to straight." She sounded close to tears. "Must I learn how to be devious and deceitful just because people can't stand the way I talk? All in the world I do that I can see is any different from anyone else is that when I think something, I come out with it. I know enough not to hurt people's feelings with frankness. That's not being straightforward, that's being cruel. I'm the way I am and I'm *not* going to make myself over for any old stuffed corset who thinks her son is Jesus Christ, when I know very well he isn't. He's just another man ... better looking than most, but he's just a man and that's all." She bent her head and a sob came from her throat.

Acy pulled her close and let her weep out her little burst on his chest. "You won't have to change, Sugar, because the best people in the world will appreciate you. What the hell do you care about a bunch of stuffed shirts and what they think. They're chaff and that's as good a way as any to find it out. You're better off every time you can brand one of 'em. He'll be out of your way then for good and all. I never liked the pup anyway."

She sat up quickly. "You mean Rod?"

"I mean Rod."

Her eyes held his for a long moment. "Acy, you wouldn't have said that if you didn't know something."

"I know plenty, Sugar, and none of it's good. However, that's not my business."

"It's my business," she said, her eyes slitting and growing hard. "If you know anything, I think you should tell me."

He shrugged. "O.K., remember, you asked for it. The boy has been in trouble with women since he was in grammar school. He has been kicked out of some of the best colleges in the country.

He drinks and fritters his time away. Never had a job in his life. In other words, he's no good."

Cyri looked away for some minutes before she spoke. "With my background, I can't say a thing about his activities with women. As for the rest, I'll have to see for myself. I'll have to find out, Acy, and I don't mean to get married or anything like that to find out. He'll have to show me what he's made of before anything gets serious. I promise you that."

"That's what I want to hear, Sugar. He's still young yet and maybe he'll snap out of it. If you're for givin' him a chance, then I am too. You work it out the best you can and I won't open my big mouth."

"I don't want it that way, Acy. I want you to open your mouth any time you feel like it. I just would like to feel that I can listen to you and use what you say in my own way."

"Your way is my way, Sugar," he said, standing up. "G'night," he slapped her seat and skipped from the room like a three year old, pausing at the doorway to make a face at her.

She rubbed her smarting behind and stuck her tongue out at him. "Just for that, no eggs tomorrow."

CHAPTER SEVEN
—AN AFFAIR ENDED

RODNEY PETTINGILL put out considerable money having the apartment cleaned, the floors waxed, the curtains laundered and the divan and chairs vacuumed. When he was done, the little apartment gleamed. Its walls were done in soft pastels with little niches and alcoves that had been regilded and silvered. There were now potted plants, new colorful slipcovers for that furniture which the cleaning could not brighten. The maple parquetry gleamed and was glassy smooth underfoot. All in all, it was a very cozy place, now that all signs of a rather slovenly Mary Jane had been cleansed away. Cyri would never let the place get in such a state, he felt sure.

He felt vibrantly confident that at last he would have a girl to whom the sharpest chick in Hollywood would have to bow down. A ripple of prickles went over him as he thought of parking with her the other night. His hand tingled when he remembered where it had been and the unearthly delight of the touch, the hungry capitulation, her stifled moans and rapid reactive movements. Only some unforeseen thing could now interfere with his plans. Feeling very light, he walked to the phone and called her.

Willie answered the phone and buzzed the upstairs three times. When he heard the click of the other phone being lifted, he put the receiver down.

"Hello, Cyri?"

"Yes, Rod?"

Was he imagining it, or was her voice just the same as when he had last called. Must be a trick of the transmission.

"Cyri, I have something to talk over with you. Could you get away this afternoon, say about four and we could eat here ... I've got a little place I use sometimes. There'd be just the two of us and I think it would be nice."

"Yes, Rod. I'd love to. Did you say four this afternoon?"

"Yes, that would give us plenty of time and you ... I mean, we'd have more time if we started early."

"Of course. I'll be ready at four."

She was and when he helped her into his convertible, his heart was pounding heavily and his stomach twisting in anticipation.

"What did your parents have to say, Rod?"

"Let's just wait till we get to my place and I'll tell you the whole thing. There's quite a lot of it."

She subsided and resolved to let him come to it by degrees. She hated to be harped at and she was not going to be guilty of it herself.

She was captivated by the apartment. "Oh, Rod, this is lovely. It is so clean and sweet smelling and the plants ... why it's almost like having a garden."

Rod busied himself mixing drinks, nodding his head. "It's all right. You like it, huh?"

"I love it. Some day I'm going to have a house in the country and it'll be all soft colors and brightness, like this."

"How'd you like to live here," he asked, taking care to make it light enough so that he could turn it into a joke if need be.

"Ummmm, I'd love it."

He handed her a drink and together they sat on the couch and Rod put his arm about her. "I like it here, too, Cyri, now that you're here." His roving eyes took in the grey gabardine dress that fit her body lovingly with just the right closeness without looking stretched to the bursting … that is, all except the area immediately below her throat, which was about as full as a dress could be.

She took off her shoes and let her nylon lacquered foot swing free, drawing the other up under her, causing the skirt to pull up and expose three inches of lusciously tanned skin. Rod's senses began to reel and the old twanging ring sounded in his ears. She acted on him like some powerful drug that he could not resist, like a quick whiff of some deadly gas, not enough to kill, but just enough to make his mind spin madly.

She finished her drink at a gulp and handed him the glass. "I think I could use another. I read too late last night and got up too early this morning. I'm kind of flat."

Her head was buzzing comfortably from the first drink, but she felt so warm and relaxed that she desired to stimulate the sense of physical freedom. The second drink, much stronger than the first, went its way and she placed the glass on a little coffee table, threw her head back, and breathed deeply. She felt uplifted, bursting with energy, reveling in her strong, healthy body that was beginning to throb with the dull pain of sensual demand. The act of taking a deep breath threw her breasts into sharp, erect prominence and Rod promptly forgot his well-planned strategy.

He wove his lips into hers, feeling the throb that fled through her and the involuntary tightening of muscles that immediately relaxed into boneless acquiescence. She went as limp as a rag and he moulded her pliant body close to his own, letting her feel the unleashed animal in him and thrilling to the restless rise of it in her.

His hands filled themselves with her bounty, wringing a deep guttural sound from her.

Rod lay beside her and drew her tenderly into his embrace and stroked the hair from her face and forehead, delighting in its deep rich smother as it lay in scattered disarray about her head and shoulders.

"I don't know why I cry when that happens," she whimpered as she put her arms around him, straining him close. "I just get so full and so overcome that I can't help it."

"It's all right, darling … it's all right." Sudden realization came to him as to what he had done and his body seemed to flame with embarrassment from ankles to scalp. He stole a look at her face and watched her lids close like mother of pearl over her eyes and the nervous thrust of her tongue as it ran over her lush red lips. At least she didn't seem to mind.

He relaxed and, placing his mouth over hers, he drew in her lower lip, then polished it lingually. She caught his upper one and repeated the operation till they both tingled with the sweetness of the act. Rod felt that he'd soon reach the bursting point because he had stretched his stamina to the very last inch. He could feel the trembling signals of returning restlessness and the whimpering affection with which she clung to him. His lips began to explore again to see the automatic arch of her back and the clonic jerk of her head.

"Oh, please, Rod, don't play any more … please. I'll die … die …"

Rod moved and to her own deep gasp, there was joined one of his own. It happened … sending little eddies of wonderment floating through the red haze of semi-conscious excitement that seemed to be drowning him, choking him with its long awaited reward.

They lay supine, dreamily resting, allowing their bodies to drink their fill of the peaceful backwaters. Cyri moved first, sitting up and surveying his well knit body as though it was something new revealed to her for the first time. She jerked slightly as a throb of memory went through her and bending, she let her heavy hair cover him as she bent forward and gathered a mouthful of taut skin and, biting it, let it escape slowly. The touch of her hair made his skin contract like the touch of a sliver of ice and Cyri, watching, was saluted, making her shudder with anticipation. Then, without quite knowing why, she surrendered to the impulse. She forced him to roll on his side, the act bringing her into ready availability, till at last there came the mutter of deep thunders and faster movement. It came in all its shadowy but cataclysmic repercussions, like some gigantic natural electrocution, in billowing rubberized clouds of soft downy nothingness on which they floated. The girl fainted momentarily, then lay as still as death, her youthful demand at long last sated to repleteness; Rod felt as though he would never be able to summon the strength to rise. Sleep crept in and fed its beneficent drug into their veins as they lay side by side ...

It was dark when they woke, Rod moving slightly to avoid waking her, but she was already awake.

"I'm awake, darling," she said, her voice rich and throaty. "I've been awake for five minutes."

He reached over and turned on a dim bedside lamp, then turned to her. "You're the most indescribable person I ever saw, Cyri." He caught her close and held her for a long time just enjoying the raptuous touch of her body, warm, vibrant and quiescent as it moulded itself to him, matching him line for line. "God, how I love you." His voice was hoarse and heavy with passion.

Her arms clutched his head with a soft pressure and the warm damp caress of her breath trickled across his neck and chest. "Rod, I never said this to another living person ... the way I mean it now. I love you and never till today did I know what the word meant. You simply have no conception of how much I love you."

"I know, darling. I know you well enough to understand that you're the sort who wouldn't say it unless that's the way you felt."

Her smile had a touch of the vixen as she said, "you know another way I feel?" With a subtle movement that revealed the strength of her youthful muscles, she showed him how she felt and the act sheeted him over with a spray of such unendurable desire that again he felt himself rocked within the cradle of wondrous motion, his already outraged muscles being whipped again into action, his ragged nerves aching, freighting heavier loads of ecstatic reaction to his brain …

Some time later, Rod chuckled and the sound had a certain mad tremble. "This could go on indefinitely, but then it can't. Limitations are limitations where humans are concerned."

Again came her vixenish smile and this time she employed her hands for a moment, then her lips, finally her hot red tongue which at last wrenched a groan from him. A rasping gasp from her came quickly and again limitations receded and widened their latitude.…

An hour later they had showered and sat in the little dinette drinking coffee after an excellent meal that had been served them by the restaurant half a block down the street. Rod spilled coffee trying to hold the cup with one hand, while Cyri's was as steady as always. She laughed aloud as he cursed and showed him the steadiness of her own hand.

"Sissy," she jibed.

Rod was not accustomed to women speaking thus boldly about things which, though they indulged, did not care to discuss afterward. He colored slightly and said nothing.

"Now that we're through eating, Rod, what did your family say?"

Rod shrugged lightly. He had looked forward to this necessity with foreboding, but since her complete capitulation, he felt better about the whole thing. All his experience had supported the concept that once they tumbled, then you could make your own rules … practically.

"Well," he began, "it's going to take time. Mother, of course, is totally without reason. Pop, on the other hand, thinks there's no one in the world quite like you. Unfortunately, after a good many years of letting her have the big say, he's sticking to the line. He won't be able to make a move without her consent. So … that leaves us right back where we started with this exception."

"What exception?" Her face hardened and her eyes grew bleak.

Rod felt a momentary pang of unease. He smiled ingratiatingly. "This …" he spread his hands. "The apartment. While we're waiting for mother to see the light there's no reason why you can't move in here. You said you'd like to live in a place like this. This is your chance."

Cyri, whose chin rested on her clasped hands, elbows on the table, did not move but her eyes gripped him. Again came the pang of fear and Rod began to elaborate on the advantages of the set up.

"With you here all the time, I could practically live here myself. We'd have all the advantages of well … married life. We could have these cozy little dinners and…. you know I love you, don't you, Cyri?" This last had been a plea squeezed out by the gradually growing realization that things were not going at all well. Something had missed, his calculations were going awry. "You do, don't you?" he prompted, his voice shredding a little.

"Let me get it straight," she said at length. "You want me to move in here?"

"That's right, Cyri. It would only be till …"

"And we would in a manner live as man and wife, is that right?"

"Yes, but only till...."

"And you say you love me?"

She stood up, her arms stiffly at her sides. "I do know. Now will you please take me home?"

"Cyri, please ..."

"You will take me home this instant or I'll walk out of here and take a taxi."

Rod, remembering the look in Acy's yellow eyes, hastened to do as she asked, being very solicitous helping her down the stairs and into the car. As they pulled away from the apartment, he tried again.

"Gosh, Cyri, I wish you wouldn't take it this way. If you don't want to stay, I'm not going to try to force you. It was just a suggestion ..."

"Please, Rod, I don't want to talk about it."

"We've got to, darling. I don't want you sore at me. I couldn't stand it like that. Tell me what I've done wrong and I'll make it up to you some way."

She faced him, sliding around in the seat to do so. "Rod, I don't pretend to understand what makes people like you and your kind tick. Acy says I can't tune in on your wave length and I guess that works both ways. I happen to know, however, that men rarely marry women who have been their mistresses. I could never lay any claim to moral excellence and I'm sure I never will. I'm just not constructed like that, but I will not become yours or any man's mistress to live in a perfect hell of love, fear, uncertainty, and scuttle here and there, keeping myself out of the public eye. With me it's either marriage or nothing. I told you tonight that I loved you. I did and I do.

"It's going to hurt me every bit as badly as it will you, and probably worse, because there are many more avenues of compensation open to men than to women. The difference in the two of us is that I've *had* to do without. I'm inoculated to it, so I can take it. You never went hungry, worked for your food, dressed in rags or less, had your youth and unworldliness imposed upon by others like I have. In any case, doing without you will just be something else I want very badly but will have to forget because I won't accept the conditions. You say you love me ..."

"Cyri," his voice had the tearing tenor of approaching frenzy, "you name your conditions, you take the wheel, just name it and you can have it. Please don't talk about us as though there wasn't any us any more. I can't stand it."

"You'd better learn how," she told him bluntly. "Because as of this night there is no more Cyri and Rod. At long last you tell me I can have everything the way I want it. Why didn't you think of that before?"

"Because it never occurred to me that you'd act like this. Please, Cyri...."

"Please nothing! You're just like the rest. You want all for nothing. I'm sick of men like you and the type of love you hand out. First you say the family won't have any, then you tell me that I can write my own ticket. What sort of double talk is that....? Don't answer. I know all too well. You meant to get everything you could for the price of that apartment which now seems hideous to me. Marriage was something that was to come if there was no other way. Maybe I'm still not very well educated to the way of the world being run, but thank heaven I found out in time. It could have been worse."

"I thought love meant something to you," he said bitterly.

"It does," she flared back. "It means so much to me that I'll put myself to torture rather than have it imposed on. I was easy, Rod. I'll admit it. That's the way I am. I enjoy my body because it is a good body and it affords me pleasures that I can't even describe, but I refuse to let it be a mat for every chance man to wipe his feet upon. It means more to me than that. I know that in some people's eyes I'm a wicked person but I don't feel that way. What I do, I do myself, I enjoy it, and I'm the one most concerned.

"You're a handsome man, Rod, and it is entirely possible that I might have agreed to come to your apartment and let you take me to the heights you did tonight without any mention of love. The word love did come up, however, and since it did, foolishly enough I suppose I expected it to mean something. I'm glad I found out before I made any bigger fool of myself."

"Suppose I'd come to you with a license and a preacher … would you reconsider?"

She thought for a while. "This has been something of a shock, Rod. It has taken something out of me that I felt for you. I can't predict anything. I don't know. All I know right now is that I don't want to see you. Not any time soon, anyway … let me out here. I want to go up the back way so I won't have to pass through the bar."

"I'll call you, Cyri." For the first time in his life the stops of humility were pulled out all the way and being so long unused they sounded a bit rusty and strange.

She looked at him for a long moment, as she stood by the curb. "I don't think I would, Rod, if I were you."

"I'll call you," he said. Humility was even more noticeable now.

She didn't answer but turned and was swallowed up in the darkness of the shadows. He strained his eyes for a last glimpse, but he saw only the nodding fronds of a large banana tree and heard the dry rustle of some of the dead leaves at its base.

Cyri undressed rapidly. This was one night when she did not want to encounter Acy who was in the habit of coming into her room, and if she hadn't gone to sleep as often was the case, he'd sit and they would talk till all hours. Cyri was wounded deeply, but she bore her hurt with a certain savage stoicism that was not unmixed with fatalism. If Rod was the way he was, then there was nothing she could do about it. She ached for him in every muscle and nerve in her body, but she was saturated with a strange and unyielding pride made all the stronger because of her background. She was a nobody, she knew that, but she was determined that she should not be treated as such. She knew she was beautiful and desirable and she wanted with an orphan's fierce yearning to be desired for herself, but not as a bit of chattel to be tossed aside at will.

She blinked her eyes hard to keep back the tears as she slipped into a pair of thin jersey pajamas, but the relaxing effect of falling into bed was more than she could resist and the tears came in a flood. They did not last long, however, because she was weary to the marrow of her bones and her body was so glutted with nerve soothing satiation, that she slipped into slumber with the tears still collected on her cheeks.

Not too long afterward, Acy tip-toed into the room and looked down on her now tranquil face. A few tears still clung to her cheeks. With meticulous care, he touched them with his handkerchief and blotted them. She stirred faintly in her sleep and took a deep sobbing breath, moaning a little as she twisted beneath the sheet and changed position. Acy turned out the bedside light that she had left on and tiptoed from the room.

"Your face," observed Willie, "portends that all is not well with the Princess."

"Nyappp," mumbled Acy, sitting in his specially built rocker. "She's been crying and she was out with that pup again. Don't know as I like it."

"I admit a similar distaste for the young gentleman. I use the term in the absence of any concrete evidence to the contrary. My intuition tells me that he lacks some of the stellar qualifications I should like to see the Princess reap should the question of marriage ever be broached."

"Y' blinkin' intuition ... y' don't even know what it is," snarled Acy, ill-temperedly.

"Intuition," Willie pointed out didactically, "is actually a misnomer. In the realm of science there is no such thing. Dr. D'Orsey contends that it is merely a subconscious evaluation of available evidence and a conscious conclusion reached thereby. Since the subject is aware of the latter and unaware of the former, he is prone to ascribe to it a certain psychic quality which it does not possess. A good term is extrasensory perception."

"Holy balls o' catfish," moaned Acy. "You pick the damndest times to run off at the mouth."

"You do not entertain any suspicion that the Princess has been badly used, do you?"

Acy shrugged. "I know she was cryin' and that means something. She ain't ... isn't the sort who weeps to hell and gone all over the place without reason. She'll fill up and run over when you do her a favor or when she appreciates somethin' a lot, but she ain't the sort to cry for nothing. Maybe she'll tell us and maybe she won't ... I don't know. Why?"

Willie stood up and his small wiry body appeared as tense as spring steel. "I should feel impelled to do some severe bodily injury to anyone who caused her pain." Acy's mouth fell open. Willie's beady black eyes flamed redly as he spoke and his hands were half clenched into claws.

"Well, I'll be a suck egg dog," breathed Acy in astonishment.

Willie, realizing that he had been somewhat swept away by his emotions, relaxed shamefacedly and sat down. "My apologies," he mumbled. "For a moment I got tuck up in …" Willie stopped and floundered helplessly.

"Well blister my bustle buttons," whispered Acy, thunderstruck. "B'goddamn if I ever heard you bust a sentence like that. You must think a lot of the Princess."

"If you will recall," murmured Willie somewhat recovered, "it was I who first discerned the fact that she was something above the average. It is true that my skin is black but that does not necessarily indicate callousness. Anyone with sufficient sensibilities to remove one's foot from a coal of fire could not see the child day in and day out for over two years and remain cold to her qualities. She is the only person I have ever known whose makeup excluded dishonesty so completely that one might say it was congenitally lacking."

"Oh, Lord, there ain't no argument there. Daisy loves the kid like a daughter, too, and I'll bet she'd claw the eyes outa anyone that done her dirt."

Willie opened his mouth to correct his employer, but closed it again, the memory of his own recent descent into the argot still fresh in his mind.

"Daisy," said Willie, massaging a certain spot on the back of his head reminiscently, "is not a woman who plays carelessly with the milk of human kindness, either. Her affection for the girl springs from the same source as ours, although she is not as prone to waste as are we."

Acy grinned, having more than a suspicion as to the source of Willie's opinion of Daisy's supply of human kindness.

CHAPTER EIGHT
—ABSALOM O'MARA

THE NEXT MORNING at breakfast, Cyri came straight to the point. "Acy, I'm not going to see that man again, in the event that you get curious when he doesn't show up any more."

He watched her attack her oatmeal with appetite, tossing back a waterfall of black hair as it slid forward and threatened to get in the way. "That's O.K., Sugar. You didn't have to tell me. Your life is your own."

"That's nice of you, Acy, but I owe too much to you to keep things like that to myself when I know you're interested. You love me, so why wouldn't you want to know?"

He waited for her to tell him why, but she went on eating. His curiosity was now aroused for certain and a knot of anger grew beneath his breast bone like a blister on a cheap tire. He didn't want to question her straight, so he went at it obliquely. "If the pup done somethin' ..."

She shook her head. "No, I want it to die quietly. Let's have no brawling or threats. What happened to me I could have prevented, but somehow ... well, I had to find out in my own way. There is some virtue in worldliness and sophistication. I have just found out."

"Some good in ever'thing, I guess," he agreed. "If not in itself, in the learnin' y' get from the experience. Thing is, don't let it beat you down. Any fool can stumble into a mud hole but not all of them can get up, wash it off and ferget it." Acy, seeing the disapproving gaze of Willie from the kitchen, cleared his throat self-consciously and averted his eyes.

That afternoon business was slack, giving Acy too much opportunity to think. Something would have to be done about Cyri. Her life was too sheltered and confined. True, she had joined a tennis club, went to the park and wore herself out three times a week on the courts, but she played with other women and refused to have anything whatever to do with them socially.

"They talk too much," she said when questioned about the attitude. "They talk about each other and speculate on who is sleeping with whom, always managing to imply that they themselves are sleeping alone. They make unkind remarks about each other all the way from who wears their pants two days without washing them, to whose brassiere contains more cotton than flesh."

Acy had retired red and sweating, leaving the girl to her opinions, never daring to urge her further toward social effort. Men, he knew, were attracted to her but were either ignored entirely or left floundering from the impact of some open faced broadside which effectively battered them into confused retreat. Some of the more persistent ones soon found that their efforts had much the same effect on her as the nibbling of a minnow on the belly of a whale. None had attempted to call because none ever succeeded in finding out where she lived and, having been reared in deviousness, they missed the simple direct method of asking her point blank … the only one that would have succeeded.

Cyri, by this time, had come to realize that her habits contained some subtle ingredient that made people squirm. Those who took her at face value were left hopelessly confused and those who thought it was a new approach, a new tangent connecting at some point to a line, were even worse off because they were wrong. It was no more than natural that she should become aware of this and use it with more objectivity than she had formerly when it was only the frank portrayal of her personality. She used it offensively and defensively, being called stupid by some, principally her female tennis partners, and complex by others, usually the frustrated males whom she left figuratively waving their hands and feet in the air like capsized tortoises.

Acy glared testily about searching for something upon which to vent his irritation. Willie, who was absently polishing the bar, caught it. "Goddammit, why'ncha change around once in a while. Y'll wear a hole in that spot."

Willie grinned irritatingly and walked the intervening distance and said, "I beg your honor's pardon, but I too was cogitating upon our problem."

"Preufff," spat Acy. "What problem?"

"That of the means to increase our lovable and seductive Princess' acquaintances and at the same time achieve it in a manner which would avoid the obvious."

Acy blinked stupidly. "Nunfff," he exploded eloquently. "Go rub a hole in the bar."

Willie departed and appeared to take the suggestion literally, obliging Acy to quell a desire to throw things and scream. With an infuriated flounce, which caused the welded joints of his chair to stretch alarmingly, he picked up an egg and shook about twice as much salt on it as he wanted. He chewed the egg with rhythmic motions of his jaws, the action forcing the fat on his face to slit his eyes and throw wrinkles into their corners.

Absalom Ventress O'Mara despised all his names, save the last, which he revered principally because it was the name borne by his great grandsire to whom legend ascribed fantastic powers with the bottle. Sean Reilly O'Mara, so the story went, could quaff half a gallon of usqueba and immediately cut a very fancy series of Gaelic dance steps. In fact, after half a gallon of usqueba, he invariably wanted to execute his dance, demanding with brazen voice and iron fists that all favored people, that being all spectators, join in thunderous applause when the dance was ended. The story also suggested that Sean always lead the applause but such stories often become less charitable as they grow older.

Ab, as he preferred to be called, had neither the titanic proportions of his revered great grandsire, nor his fabled capacity, but in all else he was a twin ... in spirit and in his own opinion. Three half-pints had been known to make Ab perform weird feats of footwork during which he held the force of gravity as nothing, but by no stretch of imagination could they be called a dance and in the end, gravity always claimed its own. There was a bumper crop of wens, bruises, scars, keloids, and other blemishes on his fair hide which bore mute evidence of the foregoing facts. Ab was stocky and, by stretching, he could top five feet ten inches. His weight vacillated from one-sixty to one-eighty, depending on whether his vitamins had been coming from bottle or food at that particular time. His face had the stout square attractiveness of a pound cake, his nose up-tilted and his bright blue eyes flashed like keen knives.

His fists carried the same quick lethal power of his vaunted ancestor, nor was Ab the least loath to use them in spite of his lack of Herculean proportions. He had the fulminating Irish temper, quick to hate and quick to forgive, romantic, emotional and effervescent.

His ready tongue and quick wit had routed him in quick stages from journalism school to advertising and thence into news reporting. Although he did well, he fell all too easily into the ways of the newsman and found it true that printer's ink gave a man a prodigious thirst. That he had had this thirst since the age of eleven fell before the providential, if spurious excuse, which newsmen invent to explain their cravings.

His Gaelic temperament was as sensitive and tender as his hair was red and he suffered his portion of a national inferiority complex which two generations of Americanism had been unable to erase from the genes of the family.

After writing three reports of his own and two rewrites for the prize cub who had an eager nose (and no experience) and a colossal crop of sand, Ab sought solace for his soul which seemed to erode more and more as time passed. He threatened to quit a dozen times, but baffled at the question as to what he would do if he did, remained to be eaten from within by a complex array of vague and indefinable gripes. He was twenty-eight and still dependent on a weekly paycheck which irked him without mercy, having, as he did, a champagne appetite, a beer income, and an eye for a dimpled knee and a pleasantly fleshed thigh.

Ab liked Acy Jones and the Old Barrel House was not too far from the press room, so it was to Acy's that his feet directed themselves automatically reacting to his thirst as the salivary glands will react to the sight of someone sucking a lemon. Moreover, his great grandfather's record still hung unblemished, a matter of some pride to Ab, but also a matter which aroused the competitor in him. He crawled up on a rococo stool, fastened his feet firmly to the brass rail and braced himself for another trial at the championship.

"The bottom of a sad, sad day to you, my svelte and sylph-like friend," he greeted Acy. "I see that thy narrow ascetic face is cut into fresh lines of pain and perseverence."

"Alliteration," Acy bit at him, "I got to take windy monologues from Willie 'cause he's wormed his way into the establishment and if I fired him I couldn't find a bungstarter or a corkscrew. From you I got to take nothin' and I ain't."

"He's bustin' out with bad grammar, Willie," tattled Ab, grinning. "You're slipping."

"The burden of my soul will roll away," sighed Willie, lugubriously, "the day he speaks a hundred words without offending the air with some rustic argot."

"Irishmen and smokes don't have souls," snarled the fat man. "All they got is a lot of brass, bull and bushwa."

"Alliteration," chided Ab. "But enough of this chit chat. I desire a fourtimer … bourbon and a glass of ice water."

Willie put the drink before him and began his endless polishing of the bar again.

"You," said Ab accusingly to Acy, "don't give a tinker's water stopper what you let drift in here, do you?"

Acy bridled instantly. "What you talkin' about?"

Ab nodded toward the end of the bar. A dark complexioned man sat there, toying with a drink and obviously admiring himself in the big mirror. He might have been described as too perfect. His hair was glistening black and seemed to have been lacquered into place with a paint gun. His clothes were too smooth and fit too well, his creases were too sharp, his shoes too bright and his tie too perfect to be true. His face had the soft olive skin and the pure sculpture of some dreamy painting. His lips were too red and his eyes too softly, smoky black.

"He pays for what he buys," said Acy shortly, actually offended as was Ab by the man's appearance.

"Know him?"

"No … don't want to know him … wish I didn't know you. Never knowed any good to come from you."

"You injure my feelings," said Ab easily. Baiting Acy was a favorite sport with him.

"Sssssstap," spat Acy, inelegantly.

"Very eloquently put," said Ab, gently. "The gentleman, I might point out is a procurer, to use the lacy term. He has stables of women. In other words, he lives off the fat of the fanny … if you follow me."

Acy squirmed. He was in a vile humor and to him a procurer was anathema even when he was in his very best mood. His mood was not improved when Cyri swung through the door clad in shorts and a striped jacket which was opened in the front to expose ivory tan skin which her halter managed to advertise rather well. Her arms held tennis balls, towel and racket.

The man swung around and let his smouldering eyes rest on her as she waved a hand at Acy and ran on through the bar and up the stairs. For a long time he watched the spot where she disappeared.

Ab let air hiss through his teeth. "You manage to keep her well hidden, Acy. I've seen her only about ten times since she's been here and every time I see her I feel as though I've been run through with one of your sabres. Speaking as a connoisseur and without the slightest intended slight, that gal has a body of the sort that has caused crowns to fall and heads to tumble gorily into wicker baskets." He downed half his huge drink and tasted his water.

Acy felt better. He liked Ab O'Mara and he always enjoyed hearing honest applause for Cyri.

"The only thing that mars an otherwise perfect entrance and exit is that our oily friend seemed to notice her too. That I do not like. I hope you'll pardon me if I confess an abiding dislike for our dear Lester, so much in fact, that in spite of never having been introduced to your protegée, I feel as though I have been personally insulted by the mere fact that he looked at her."

"You talk too much," asserted Acy, comfortably as he salted an egg, "and you don't never say nuthin.… anything."

Ab emptied his drink and cooed unintelligibly at Willie to whom the coo was quite intelligible.

Ab drank half his new drink and lit a cigarette. "To pursue a favorite topic of mine, I happened to be at night court once when Lester came to bail out a baker's dozen of his meal tickets. That's how I happened to know about him. I heard one of the gay girlies call him something which I would repeat to you, knowing your own flair for picturesque patter, were I the sort who would sully my lips with such. I became interested and spoke to Tully Istre, who knows everything about everybody. Tully unloaded and I felt so ill I had to take a shower."

"Probably needed it," hazarded Acy, nastily.

"Disrespect," murmured Ab, abstractly. "Total disrespect. As I was saying, Tully gave me the lowdown. Lester has other interests, none of which are savory. For a price, he will slip you an address which leads to a horrid old witch whose livelihood is that of taking the lives of young frightened girls in her filthy hands for a good stiff price. He steers people to cesspools of whatever choice their taste demands and in this town, my skinny friend, that connotes latitudes which make even this sophisticated Irishman blanch. It is reliably reported that Lester himself cares not a whit for natural methods of escapism and many have been the suggested avenues he adores. Speculation, certainly, but indicative of something. It has been one of my more ignoble yens to find out what." Ab cooed again and Willie obliged.

Acy was interested in spite of himself. "Would he be Lester Lamb, by any chance?"

"I'd say purely by chance. Surely he isn't Lester Lamb by intent. Who, in their right mind, would deliberately ..."

"Heard of him," said Acy, his face growing darker. "Scorpion, gutted amaryllis."

Ab emitted a gusty haw. "That's why I love you, Acy. You concoct such original opprobrium."

"The gentleman," put in Willie in a hushed voice, "is drinking Queen's Clamors."

"Arrrgh," shuddered O'Mara. "What would go into a Queen's Clamor?"

"Light rum, cointreau and orange bitters," answered Willie with a visible shudder. "I become ill concocting them."

"Small wonder." Ab was becoming a little drunk. "Acy, what are you going to do with the girl?"

"Problem," muttered Acy, salting an egg. "Problem. I feel guilty hiding her here ... as it were. She seems as happy as any healthy kid, though. It ain't showin' none."

"Er ... I beg your pardon." The voice was fruity and rich, unctious and threaded through with a husky caress.

Acy glared and Ab turned slowly, as though expecting to find Lester at his elbow. He found him and inspected him as one would something spewed up on a beach from the depths.

"Yeah," Acy was glassy hard.

"Er ... the lady who went upstairs a while ago. She interests me strangely."

"I dare say," answered O'Mara brightly. "One gathers that if she interested you it would be strangely, very strangely and doubtless revolting."

Lester ignored the reporter as though he didn't exist. "I should like to be introduced to her, a really beautiful girl ... really."

"Willie," Acy's voice was barely under control, "what does *this* owe?"

"Four eighty, sir."

"Four eighty," said Acy, holding out a hand the size of a wedding cake.

"Oh … certainly." He handed over the money. "Now about the girl …"

"Would you like to go out the same way you came in, or would you prefer to be assisted?"

A shadow crossed the man's face. "I asked about the girl, that dream with legs and clinging shorts. As of now, I haven't been answered."

"Your answer, Lester," put in O'Mara sliding slowly down from his stool, "was specific directions to the door."

Acy was gradually turning purple, his big hands balled up before him like twin mortar shells but he made no answer.

Lester sighed regretfully. "I am not accustomed to trifling. I made a request and so far I've been given hostile stares and considerable stupid chaff."

"Tell me, Lester," chortled Ab, moving slightly away from his stool. "What makes you think you can demand an introduction to a man's daughter when he obviously would like you only under one condition … dead?"

"The girl is not his daughter. She is a waif, brought to the city by a friend of mine and forcibly taken from him. She is a murderess and she occupied this man's couch …" There was a sudden flurry of action, a sharp crack and Lester struck the floor resoundingly, skidded swiftly along, picking up a great deal of sawdust, a spittoon, a chair and fetching up well under the table of a nearby booth. For a good three minutes he stayed in the position, raised somewhat on his hands, his head hanging and his hair now disordered and stringing. He shook his head several times and then laboriously crawled out from under the table.

Acy laughed deep in his belly like a brick rolling around in an empty oil drum. "Willie, set Mr. O'Mara up with his usual and it's on the house. Hot damn, if I ever seen … saw a sweeter left hook. Didn't think you had it in ye, bub."

Ab sat back on his stool and flexed the fingers of his left hand, eyeing them with amazed gratification. "There is no satisfaction quite like swatting a dog, Acy. However, I'll accept your treat and changed attitude … The door, Lester, is in the same place it was when it was first showed you."

Lester came unsteadily to his feet. "I think," he said slowly, "you will both be sorry."

"I should be," chuckled Ab, equably. "As happy as I am right now, it would be no more than fair."

Lester straightened his tie, ran trembling fingers through his hair, brushed some of the sawdust from his elegant suit and let his soft eyes rest on O'Mara. "I shall be delighted to attend to it … Mr. O'Mara, I believe?"

"Oh quite, quite and all that sort of Thomas rot. However, Lester, I think it only fair to tell you that as much as I enjoyed caressing you in the kisser, I'd enjoy it even more the next time and I assure you I'll do a better job next time. Onward ever, backward never, I always say."

Lamb nodded gently. "Yes … I'll remember." He walked out of the bar on legs that were rather rubbery.

Ab sighed happily. "Now I know how St. George felt when he slew the dragon. Oh, I might mention, Acy, that the man has a staff of hoods and I think he was stung in a very sensitive spot. He might try retaliatory measures."

Acy shrugged heavily. "Son, I been here thirty years. I been threatened before. Better look out for him yourself."

"I will. Now that my brain has cleared somewhat, I wonder if it's safe to go home … Oh, what the hell did he mean about her being a murderess and …" Ab stopped, unwilling to finish it.

Acy was silent for a moment. "Can't say … won't say. It's her secret and if she tells you …"

"Then there is something?"

"Something," admitted Acy, chopping off the word. "Just what … I ain't sayin'."

"Sorry … I didn't mean to pry, but when the blankety blank said that, I guess I went off my rocker momentarily. Whatever it is, I'm on the kid's side. If she's a murderess then I'm Lester Lamb."

Acy nodded. "Yeah!"

Ab finished his drink and eyed his glass morosely. "Acy, are you sensitive about that kid or are you just particular about who you introduce to her?"

"There's been a couple of scabs like Lester who wanted to meet her and they got just what he got, only I don't move about as rapid as you and I might have been a little clumsy. She's had dates and I never raised my voice. I don't aim to build no fence around her."

Ab nodded with slow, positive motions. "Laudable attitude. I wonder if I might meet her … sometime. Sometime when I'm sober."

"I'd be glad to have you meet her," Acy's manifest sincerity made a tingle touch O'Mara's breast.

"Thanks, Acy. You don't hand 'em out and I don't want 'em … compliments, I mean. I guess we understand each other."

"Probably, but just to go on record, Ab, I'd better tell you right at the start, that kid is into me like a fish hook. If you ever cause a tear to come to her eyes, you'll be a hell of a lot sorrier than Lester Lamb could ever make you."

Ab drained his glass and put it down carefully. "I believe you and you have my word. I don't mind telling you that she has a fish hook in me, too. Has ever since I first saw her, but I'm not the guy for her, Acy. I've got a snake eating away inside me and the only thing that stops it is bourbon. She deserves better than that … even as a companion."

"She deserves more'n any man I know can furnish," said Acy in a hard voice, "but what she wants is the only thing I'm concerned about. Butterflies ain't too partickler ... particular about what they light on, you know ... you, a flower, anything."

Ab stood down from the stool. "I think I'll go home and sober up. I'll be back tomorrow."

"Watch your step," advised the fat man.

Ab reeled, but caught himself in time. "Sure ... sure. Reminding me of Lester when I'm gonna meet the most beautiful girl in the world tomorrow ... hah! Crepehanger!" Ab walked unsteadily through the door and was swallowed up by the night.

"Put yer intuition to work on him," said Acy, challengingly.

Willie pursed his lips and thought for a moment. "A gentleman, sir. A real gentleman. A man who is all fire and acid, a man who honors women ... probably because he loved his mother a great deal." He paused and folded a bar rag. "A very unhappy man."

"How d'ye know?"

"Intuition, perhaps. His er, blarney and glib speech are a front, extroverted to such a marked degree that one suspects that it hides introversion to an even greater degree. A remarkable example of compensation."

"Never mind the hooraw, can we approve of him for Cyri?"

"I should say so. He is an extraordinary man."

Acy slipped into his old habit. "Pup ... impertinent pup. Spurifft ... damned nuisance."

Willie grinned enigmatically and put away his bar rags for the night, then reaching into a small hidden cubicle, he withdrew a long barreled .22 automatic.

"What are you going to do with that water pistol?" Acy wanted to know.

Willie thrust it into his waistband under his shirt and walked around the end of the bar. "Intuition working further suggests that pugnacious news reporter might find short shrift should the minions of evil be abroad in the form of Mr. Lamb's hoods. I think a shadow half a block in the rear might prove fortuitous."

Acy nodded, his eyes slitting. "Go ahead. I'll close up." Acy had seen too much evidence of Willie's so called intuition to treat it lightly. There were times when the black man seemed to be in close communion with dark forces which have been the guardians of his race for eons.

Absalom O'Mara walked up Bourbon toward Canal Street feeling too rosy and lightfooted to worry overmuch about Lester Lamb. In fact, he had forgotten Lamb entirely, thinking of the morrow when he was to finally meet Cyri. His mind was in a modest turmoil over the projected meeting because Ab had been in love with Cyri for more months than had been comfortable, especially to a man whose romanticism had elevated the girl to such a position that he felt unworthy of her. He inclined toward a low opinion of himself and lay all his accomplishments on the line. For his future possibilities he stuck a thermometer into the bowels of his intelligence. Man, when in the throes of this sort of malady, finds the simplest things distorted past all recognition so his stock taking, after full evaluation, is below a quotable minimum.

When he first saw her, he was drunk already and from past experiences assumed that she was his unconscious seizing a medium upon which it could build everything that O'Mara had ever desired. The next three times he saw her, he was sober and after that, he saw her in both states, all of which served to intensify his original assessment.

Ab, contrary to public opinion and supporting Willie's theory, was essentially a shy man, especially where certain types of women were concerned. Cyri had looked into his eyes once and O'Mara hadn't recovered for days. Shy people usually prefer the windows of their souls to remain closed, save to a favored and deserving few, and Ab felt that in one glance Cyri had unshuttered every window in his house. He actually conceived a fear of her and it was only after several more sights of her that he gradually reached the firm conviction that here, at long last, was a woman with whom a man could afford to bare himself and suffer no damage. It is a peculiarity of the shy person that they will, when assured of understanding, open their hearts with a rush and their reticence is a result of fear of hurt.

Ab, once he had established confidence in her, began to plot strategy to the end of meeting her. Now that the meeting was assured, his shyness again came to the fore, resulting in the inventory which in persons of his temperament is likely to be disparaging.

Ab stopped and looked in the show window of an antique shop and pondered over the propriety of giving her a present. He was still looking and pondering when a short, but expertly wielded length of lead pipe descended on his head and, as he fell, a boot of unnecessarily large proportions dug itself in his side. He therefore did not hear the rapid, spiteful rattle of a .22 automatic.

Mack Pitre heard it ... and felt it ... One leg crumpled under him with disconcerting suddenness and he felt several blows about the shoulders and chest.

Lester Lamb heard it, too and seeing Mack Pitre fold up on the sidewalk, gunned the motor of his car, intent on leaving the scene with all speed, when there came to his ears the menacing snap of a small calibre bullet daintily accompanied by the tinkle of falling glass. Lester's foot bore down heavily on the accelerator, making his subsequent wreck all the more devastating. A bullet coming through the back glass, already flattened with much of the force taken from it, struck him just above the ear and tore a ragged uneven furrow around his head, coming to a stop at the hairline near his forehead. The car went out of control and attempted to climb a stout brick wall, fell back and skidded in a tight circle, coming to rest wearily against the steel trunk of a lamp post.

Police whistles shrilled and minions of the law converged on the spot with drawn weapons. They examined O'Mara who was, for some reason not at the moment ascertainable, unconscious, grinning, but breathing steadily. Mack Pitre was neither grinning nor breathing with any degree of ease or regularity due to the amount of blood that threatened momentarily to choke him.

One policeman went to a call box for an ambulance while the first to arrive on the scene wrote laboriously in a notebook, cursing the apparent lack of witnesses.

At this point a small, dapper, colored man approached the scene. "Good evening, officer. There seems to be a shambles here."

The policeman blinked unbelievingly, then grinned. "Evenin', Willie … where'n hell you pop from? I thought you'd be at the bar feeding Acy boiled eggs."

Willie shrugged. "Not much business tonight, sir. We closed early and I came out for a constitutional."

The officer laughed aloud. Willie's speech being much better than his own intrigued him. "See any of this?"

"Submit, sir, that I saw it all."

"What? The hell you did. Where was you?"

"Request most earnestly that respected employer not be informed of the fact, but I must confess that after the first shot I discovered that in some manner I had become jammed rather tightly beneath yonder parked automobile, a reflex you might call it, sir … sorry I'm sure. If Mr. Jones should hear of it I should have to endure months of chaffing."

The officer now joined by the second, burst into a gale of laughter which the other joined.

"Now," said the former, wiping his eyes, "tell me what you saw."

"Well, sir, I was some distance behind Mr. O'Mara here ..."

"Hell's bells." The policeman directed the beam of his torch at the prone figure of O'Mara. "Didn't reckernize him at first ... Him all right ... go on, Willie."

"Well, we walked along separated by some distance, Mr. O'Mara had, er, a considerable cargo tonight and I was afraid he'd fall and hurt himself ..."

"Snootful," said the second officer. "Always ..."

"Yes, sir ... a car drove up and this large gentleman got out." He indicated the bubbling figure with a slim forefinger. "He approached Mr. O'Mara, who was at the time inspecting the contents of this window, with what appeared an avid eye, and was struck from behind without seeing his assailant. Almost immediately from a position behind me ... I regret to say I didn't even look in that direction when I dived beneath the car ... there arose a fusilade of fire. The gentleman there fell wounded and the occupant of the car started away, only to become a victim of the gunfire before he had gone fifty feet."

As Willie spoke, the officer with the notebook wrote furiously. "Now, Willie, you say you didn't look behind you where the gunfire was coming from?"

"No, sir. At that precise moment I fear I was zealously removing myself from the sphere, away from any possible stray bullet."

The officers laughed and the first one asked, "You don't recall any other little detail ... anything else that might give us a lead on the gunman?"

Willie seemed to hesitate. "Well, sir, this is only a rather nebulous impression, but I seem to recall a passing flicker of wonderment because of the reports. I thought of a silencer, but they were a little too sharp for that. None of the dull grunt as one hears from a silencer. The cracks were keen and sharp. I thought of a .22 but that would be a silly thing ..."

Both policemen uttered oaths and bent over Mack Pitre, examined him quickly, then stood up.

"You were right, Willie," said the first policeman. "Anyone going on the prod with a .22 must either be crazy or a trick shot. Looks like this one could have cut a playing card edgeways at twenty paces."

"What," added the second, "about popping the guy in that moving automobile at ... Let's see ... hell about seventy five yards at a guess. That's the car you were in, eh, Willie?"

"*Under,* sir. Yes, sir."

"Unh hunh. That's forty yards and if it came from behind you ... fifty yards at the least."

The policeman who had first come on the scene beckoned to Willie. "Come 'ere, Willie. I want to pat you down. Not that I suspect you, but ..." Willie stepped up obediently and was declared clean. "O.K., just wanted to make sure ... there's the ambulance. Damn, it's a little one ... what the hell, didn't you tell 'em it was three men?"

"Sure ... as usual, they were half asleep."

A patrol car pulled up ahead of the ambulance and two plain clothes men got out. "What's up, Mike?"

The first officer pointed with his night stick. "Two wounded men and a cosh, sir."

The detective sneered. "Too much Edgar Wallace, Mike ... who's the shine?"

"Acy Jones' boy."

"Oh, didn't recognize you, Willie ... How's Acy?"

"Very well, Lieutenant. We haven't had the pleasure of your company lately."

"Unh hunh ... say, how're three men going to get in that roadster?"

"Only one available, sir," said the white-coated ambulance attendant. "Seven car wrecks within the last hour. Belt of fog up around Moissant Airport and the overpass. Bad for driving."

"Beg your pardon, Lieutenant," said Willie. "Mr. O'Mara doesn't seem to be hurt too badly and we have plenty of room. I suggest that you put him in the patrol car and take him to our place. Dr. Bannerman lives in an apartment next door and we could wake him."

The lieutenant looked at the ambulance driver questioningly.

"Good idea, sir. We're run ragged tonight and we'll be sure to have other calls when we get back. If they can take care of him it might save someone's life. He just got a conk and a gash in his head."

Acy, draped in a night shirt that might have served as a small sideshow tent, opened the door and peered out as Lieutenant Eccles and Sargeant Micheals brought O'Mara up the steps to the back entrance, with Willie carrying the feet.

Acy glowered. "Whatcha y' got there, Charley?"

Lt. Eccles grimaced. "One of your customers. That's what happens to 'em when they load up on your joy juice."

"Bring 'im on in. Willie, how'n hell did you get messed up in it?"

"Begging your honor's pardon, the matter was wholly involuntary ... and discommoding."

"I didn't know you was ever a judge," grinned Micheals.

"Fappp," exploded Acy. "That's just another of Willie's titles ... consarn him."

Cyri appeared, wrapped in a dark green robe through the folds of which flashed glimpses of leg, knee and thigh, her hair wild and disordered, but enticing as ever. "What happened, Acy?"

"O'Mara got coshed."

"Another Edgar Wallace fan," moaned Eccles. "Where's this doctor you were talking about, Willie?"

"I shall depart with all speed and return with same," said Willie as he dusted off his snappy black hat and put it on his head.

"Lieutenant Eccles ... Sargeant Micheals ... my ward, Miss Malnoir."

Cyri smiled at them briefly and acknowledged their mumbled words of greeting. Micheals gasped from an elbow as Eccles poked him and realized he had been gaping. Eccles then turned to the job himself.

The girl bent over the unconscious O'Mara and tenderly pulled locks of red hair from the wound. "Acy, get a fresh wash cloth and a basin of water. I can have this ready when the doctor comes."

Fifteen minutes later, Dr. Bannerman, fat and puffing, came in. He was dressed in pajama coat and hastily donned pants with gallusses trailing behind him in graceful loops.

"Sorry ... pretty slow when I'm waked at this hour. Hope he's near death, otherwise I'm gonna be mad ... Hummm, nice job, Cyri. Might have known you did it. Rest here ain't got enough sense."

Twenty minutes later with twenty stitches in his head, O'Mara slept comfortably in Cyri's sweetly perfumed bed.

Acy fumed in the living room. "He coulda took my bed, Sugar. This here couch ain't no place for a tender pullet like you to lay her body."

"Quiet," she ordered. "You couldn't even have stayed on the couch, much less slept there." She stretched healthily and her round firm limbs slithered about beneath the silk of her pajamas in a manner that made Acy undergo another spasm of acute aching love for this delightful waif that fate had placed in his care.

Willie came in and sat on his stool, mopping his brow. "The heat is most enervating tonight."

"Talk," snarled Acy. "What happened?"

Willie lifted his shoulders a little. "As I anticipated, he was attacked. I was too far to do anything immediately, but before his assailant could run, I squirted a little water on him. The other gentleman ... the lacquered one, Mr. Lamb, was nearby in a car. I took a couple of quick snaps at him and the last shot luckily went home and his car rammed a building, skidded and came to a stop against a lamp post. He was doggo until the police had a chance to arrive on the spot."

"Where's your gun?"

"Imminent possibility of being searched made it necessary to cache same. I dashed back and picked it up. I have but just returned."

"Smart boy. Was you searched?"

Willie nodded. "Even as I anticipated."

Cyri sat up and rubbed her back against the plush of the couch. The effort caused her sharply erect breasts to behave disconcertingly under the thin covering of her pajamas. "Mr. O'Mara ... Acy, he has a funny face."

Acy and Willie exchanged quick looks. "What's funny about it, Sugar?"

"I don't know. It's sort of devilish, humorous in a way. He isn't at all handsome, but he's still attractive. Somehow, I'll bet he's a lot of fun."

"Like to meet 'im, Sugar?"

She smiled. "I can hardly help it, can I? He's here for a while if the doctor's right."

Acy nodded. "Guess so. Wonder if he has any relatives."

"Judging from maudlin confession to which I once listened," said Willie, "I'd say no. He comes from a small town upstate. Evergreen, I think he said. He didn't mention family. Other statistics gathered were, four years at Louisiana State University, where he was enamored of a campus queen whom it appears and I quote, 'Couldn't see me for the fog of male ants on the way to the honey.' "

A shadow passed over Cyri's face. "I sensed somehow that he had been hurt. Maybe that's it."

"A man like him can recall all sorts of hurts when he's tight," remarked Acy. "I oughta write a book."

CHAPTER NINE
—A NURSE IN LOVE

A BSALOM O'MARA was frightened. He was encased in a cyclonic mass of blackish foggy substance, whirling around at dizzying speed. Gradually he began whirling with it until at last he was spinning at the same speed of the dreary medium. Faster and faster it whirled till he felt himself squirted upward with terrifying speed through a tiny funnel-mouthed object, then all was light.

He found himself sitting up in a strange room, his face and body drenched with the sour sweat of horror. He controlled his breath after a bit and took stock of his surroundings. The room was large and decorated with that carelessly strewn fashion that makes for comfort and hominess. There were two large, comfortable chairs, modern and upholstered, a dressing table with three mirrors, of intricately carved rosewood and tastefully draped at the bottom in colorful print. Soft light shone from an antique brass lamp with a hand-painted parchment shade. It rested on a tall, massive walnut chest containing numerous drawers. On the floor was a dark blue carpet which harmonized in friendly fashion with the sky blue lining of the tester over his head. The bed was walnut also, but where the chest was carved, the bed was severely simple, but massive in design. It was, he decided, large enough for about four people. The walls shone richly in the dim light, cream colored and paneled three feet from the floor in dull finished walnut. It was a cheery room but somewhat elegant in a restrained way. It reminded him of two ages joining hands without conflict.

He took three Kleenex napkins from the bedside table and wiped his face, his hand trembling, his stomach jerking from nervousness. His hand touched a bandage and he felt of it gingerly, becoming gradually aware that his head was one great dull ache. His memory was none of the best at best and what with the liquor he had consumed and the subsequent buffet on the skull, things were in turmoil. He remembered drinking and finally recalled lowering the boom on someone, but after that the turmoil took over and he squeezed his eyes shut trying to put his thoughts in order. He tossed the used tissues into the refuse bucket near the night table, and, in so doing, overturned a glass of water which struck the metal receptacle sending up a hellish clatter.

Almost instantly, it appeared, Cyri stepped gracefully through the door. Her soft masses of hair were disordered, tumbling wildly about her shoulders, and the dark pools that served her for eyes were smoothly heavy from slumber. Her smile had a warm maternal quality which, along with her overwhelming beauty, made O'Mara feel suddenly stifled.

"So you finally waked," she said. "The doctor said you would."

Ab swallowed and strove to catch enough of his fleeing senses to make a coherent reply. The nearness of her, the subtle perfume of her clean, young body as she stood at the bedside, the open house coat revealing smudged suggestions of her lithe body, the efforts of her sharp breasts to pierce the thin jersey of her pajama coat, and her absolute unconcern about the matter, made his fair face flame and the suffocating hand grip his throat tighter.

"Yeah," he croaked. "What happened?"

"Some man struck you on the back of the head about three blocks from Canal. Willie shot him and another man and the police took over. They didn't know Willie shot them."

"They didn't, huh? I suppose Willie didn't want the police to know he shot them."

"I'm sure he didn't, else he'd have told them."

O'Mara looked at her queerly. "What do you suppose a man wanted to conk me for?"

"They told me," she said, sitting on the side of the bed, "that you struck a man named Lamb because he said something uncomplimentary about me. I want to thank you. I appreciate that more than you know, but I wish you hadn't."

Ab's eyes popped. "Why, for crice sake? You mean you wouldn't want me to stop a man of his sort talking about you?"

"No, not that. You see, he was telling the truth."

Ab gasped. "He ... you mean ... Hell, woman, it couldn't be true."

"But it is."

Ab gripped the cover. "Now wait a minute. The man said you were a murderer and that you occupied the ..." He stopped, his face growing red again.

"I'm a murderer in a sense, Mr. O'Mara. And the other thing is also true. If I have any defense at all it is that I was young and I didn't know anything." She told him the story of her father and this time she managed to use a few euphemisms. Ab's face was white when she was through.

"You poor kid ... you poor, poor kid. I didn't know such people ... hell, yes I did know it, but how in the world anyone could do that to *you,* I can't see. Couldn't he see ..." He stopped. Everyone should be able to see it because it was there in every glorious line of her, in her honesty, her ability to sit there and discuss it as dispassionately as though it had happened to someone else.

He shook his head. "I know the world and the more I know, the less I like." He touched her hand with gentleness and compassion, half expecting her to withdraw it. She did no such thing, but turned it over and grasped his own.

"Don't let my troubles bother you, Mr. O'Mara. They're gone and forgotten except when someone like Lamb who found out in some manner, brings it up. I'm happy now and the old life is just something to help me enjoy this one by contrast."

Ab's wonderment grew by the minute. "It seems you'd hate men after all that. First your father betrayed you, then this … this … whoever he was. God! It's a wonder you can sit here and …" He looked about the room. "You gave up your room to me, didn't you?"

She smiled and nodded. "I just loaned it to you. When you're able to get up, I'll take it back."

He shook his head. "After all that men have done to you, you can still be kind to someone you never met. You must be a bit of all right inside."

"I never let things upset me to the point of losing my sense of balance, humor, or judgment. That is, I haven't yet. Maybe I will someday, but so far I've managed to stay on top."

"You will too," he promised seriously. "My Dad told me something once that I don't think I fully understood till now. He said, 'Ab, it ain't what you do that's really bad, it's the effect it has on you. If it can't reach you, then it can't hurt you.' All these things never reached you, Cyri, so they never hurt you, yet you aren't what we usually call hard. You're just rugged. There're no weak timbers in your makeup." Her smile made his heart race madly and she squeezed the hand which she still held.

"Thanks a lot for that, Ab … I'm going to call you Ab."

He nodded vigorously. "I meant to tell you that. I hope we can be the best of friends."

She slipped off the bed and stood beside him. "You don't mean that, Ab ... do you? What you really mean is that you hope we can be much more than the best of friends."

Ab's face purpled with embarrassment. It was exactly what he had meant, but he hadn't intended for her to know it yet, but shyness admires frankness and Ab felt a glow, a deep seated warmth that burned like a strong drink on an empty stomach.

His grin was personable. "O.K. then, Miss Mind Reader, I do."

"Can I get anything for you?"

He shook his head slowly as his mind raced to one thing she could do and stopped short, with an inaudible crash as it were. "No ..."

Cyri, whose eyes still retained a great deal of their childhood penetration, read his mind with the same ease with which she had read it previously. What simple things men are, she thought, as she examined the rapt and hungry look on his face.

Her smile was faint but tender, and bending she kissed him lightly, like the touch of an angel's wing tip, on the lips. Her own were warm and sweet, leaving a little spot of dampness that cooled and remained long after she had floated through the door leading to the living room.

Ab touched his lip, withdrew his hand and gazed at it as though it had offended him in some way, then lay carefully back, sinking into the coolness of the downy pillow. He and love had been quits ever since his college days, and though his life was spotted with many an idle five minutes, he had never allowed the time to extend itself into anything approaching permanence. Occasionally, he would return for another five minutes, but even so, he never permitted any confusion regarding goals. This attitude had reaped Ab many fast friends among the female sex, but assignations weren't as frequent as they might have been had he used the age old weapon with which men are accustomed to storming feminine citadels. He made love lightly, but he was not a man who played lightly with love. There was, in his estimation, a vast difference.

Just how long O'Mara lived in saturation of the memory of Cyri's light, but ineffably sweet kiss, he had no way of determining; but the sun, glowing red about the spire of the St. Louis Cathedral, and painting a futuristic canvas through the venetian blinds on the creamy wall, drew his attention away from the magic touch. His head throbbed only occasionally now and he was conscious of a numbing evanescent lassitude stealing into his body, a feeling that prohibited movement and made even the twitching of a finger seem too much trouble to attempt.

He had to call the office because this was his morning to appear at seven and though the sun was coming up early now … He sat up at the thought and fought off an attack of dizziness, then eased his feet from the bed. He could see the phone on a small table near the chest so he made his way carefully to it and sat heavily on the small stool. He called the city editor at his home, who answered, disgruntled at the early call, till he heard what O'Mara had to say.

"You say he conked you … you mean …"

"Look," said O'Mara, wearily, "I told you and I'm not repeating it. I've got a gash in my head as long as the Basin Canal and I'm weaving about here on this damn stool. I've given you the pith of the matter and if you can't get some dope to make a story out of it, then you need to go back to school, if, indeed, you ever went, which I have reason to doubt. It was Lamb and his boys. I wiped up the Old Barrel House with him last night and that was his revenge. He and a henchman were rather well taken care of by … well, someone whose name need not appear."

"You mean," screeched the editor, "you know the man's name and you ain't tellin'?"

"I ain't tellin'," snarled Ab. "I might need him again and I never look a gift rescuer in the mouth." He hung up on a flood of despairing sulphurous language and started back to the bed. He made the first two steps very well, then he did a reverse passage through the funnel into the black mist and knew no more till he woke up with his head in Cyri's warm, enveloping lap. She was bathing his face and forehead with a cold cloth, tender and soothing of touch, but hard of eye.

"Who told you to get out of that bed?" she scolded, her eyes flashing, her beautifully rounded breasts heaving.

"Had to," he said, humbly managing a weak grin. "Got a job I have to keep."

"Your immediate job is to get well. You may have a fractured skull and until the doctor can X-ray you, you'll have to stay in bed."

"He can't x-ray me here," argued Ab, reasonably.

"He can in his office next door and you can be carried there on a stretcher. One more trip like this and I'll open the other side of your head."

"From your white and delicate but facile hands, honey chile, it would be a positive pleasure."

For a moment her face was blank, then she smiled. "You're kidding. I said you'd probably be a lot of fun."

Ab perked up. "You did? Who to?"

"Acy. I told him last night."

"What'd he say?"

She frowned a little, thinking. "I don't remember … Oh, yes, he asked me if I wanted to meet you."

"Do you?"

"I already have."

Ab chuckled. "By golly, that's right, you have, and now that you have, what do you think of me?"

She cocked her head on one side with mock seriousness. "Now, I don't know. You're stubborn, hard-headed, full of wind, water, and waste … but you're sort of cute in an ugly way. I still think you'd be fun."

O'Mara squirmed uncomfortably. Though he half suspected her of kidding, there was a serious note to her voice and her character analysis came a little too close for comfort. "Well, I've been called a lot of things, but never cute."

"Don't let it get you down … I said, in an ugly sort of way."

"Dad rat it, I heard you. Why did you have to put it that way?"

Her voice softened. "You know I'm kidding, Ab. You're just as cute as a ten day old pup … Pit bull."

He grinned and sat up. "I think I could get back in bed now." With her help, he managed it and lay there with memories of the last five minutes eating their way into his brain like an army of delightful worms. His neck still tingled from the contact of her soft skin, yet he knew that under that skin played long symmetrical muscles that were conditioned finely, that were strong, as proved by the extraordinary strength with which she almost lifted him into the bed.

Once, while she was holding his head in her lap, his cheek had touched her stomach which was also soft but firm. A shocking spray of tingles raced over his body like the burn of a carbonated drink as he recalled the caress of her hair on his face and neck as she let him back slowly on his pillow. Ab, having forgotten to breathe while under the anesthesia of her closeness and its memories, now gasped deeply for breath and fought off another spell of dizziness.

"You'll have a good breakfast in an hour," she had promised. "Then by the time you're through, the doctor'll see you again."

Ab almost counted the minutes which dragged and dragged till he was sweating with impatience. He was hungry, too. He had not eaten since noon of the previous day and the pit of his empty stomach gnawed with a dull pain as did his head.

Finally she came, bearing a tray. She had dressed in cool, crisp print that was cut square at the neck and fell somewhat off the shoulders, exposing a great deal of satiny skin which had been kissed tawny by the sun.

"Even the sun loves you," he breathed with a humility and adoration which ran a quick knife of feeling deep into the girl's breast.

She smiled mistily as she put the tray in his lap. "Ab, you have such a lot of sensitivity." She sat down and bathed him in the light of her eyes. "You feel things quickly and deeply and when you do, it comes out ... and if it didn't, I'd know because it shows on your face."

Ab paused in the act of adding thick cream to his coffee and gave her another of his queer, half fearful glances. "And you, my elegant, know too damn much for anyone's comfort."

She frowned. "That's something I don't understand about people. Why should my knowing things like that make people uncomfortable? I mean no harm. I wouldn't knowingly hurt anyone. I told you about me last night ... things I have learned will make people recoil with horror, things that will make people feel that I'm dirty and terrible. Why should you mind if I notice something about you and say so?"

He shrugged as he buttered his crisp, soft-centered rolls. "Honey, there's no way that I can explain it to you. I'm ashamed of my part of it. From now on, I'll be your little laboratory animal. Dissect me at will and I'll bear up as best I can. As for what you told me last night, I only felt sorry for you when you had been misused. I think you are neither dirty nor terrible."

"Suppose," she said in a dead, heavy voice, "I told you I enjoyed all of it, that I feel no sense of wrong and that I seem to be a person whose bodily demand must be fed?"

Ab cut into the luscious omelette and took a bite, along with half a buttered roll. He took a sip of rich, fragrant coffee and masticated. "Suppose I told you that I was the same way?" he countered.

"I know men are that way and yet women aren't supposed to be. Why, Ab?"

"Again you have me. It lacks physical reason, it lacks common, ordinary barnyard justice, and appears to have been something which men started for a reason that loses more and more logic the longer it exists."

She was silent till he had finished his rather large breakfast.

"Now," he said lightly. "If I could have another cup of coffee, I'd be glad to return that kiss you gave me this morning."

Her smile was so brilliant that he felt a little scorched. She skidded from the bed and ran out of the room with the light, sure tread of a dancer.

Such a wave of blinding emotion went over him at that moment that he felt he'd be ill and lose his breakfast. He was too highly strung to mix emotion and the mundane but necessary acts like eating. He recalled his father's cast iron ban on any unpleasantness at meal times, and thought it was a good idea. Unpleasantness can have the same effect as sudden overpowering emotion.

She returned with his coffee and watched him as he drank it slowly. It was quite hot. He felt naked and under a microscope as she watched, and made a resolution that here was one case when he'd better play it right because there was no such thing as keeping things from her. Her mind was too keenly alert, her reactions too unfettered and true and his Gaelic map too revealing.

He finished the coffee and handed her the cup, having forgotten about his bargain because, although he would have liked to kiss her above all things, his remark had been banter and nothing else. Again he was treated to the manner in which Cyri's mind worked in its purely objective manner.

She put the cup on the night table and sat on the bed again, quite close to him. He was, for a moment, nonplussed and must have shown it. Her eyes were shadowy pools of heartbreaking loveliness and at this close range he could see the exquisite texture of her skin and the damp lushness of her lips.

"I want my kiss back," she murmured, seeing that he was taken a little aback.

A grin broke out on his face like a fire in dry tinder and this time there was none of the butterfly brush-off kiss. He caught her in his arms, noticed with a quick, almost painful pang, that she came to him without even a suggestion of resistance and his lips melted into hers like they had always belonged there. O'Mara was not in the kind of physical condition that could accept calmly the warm sweetness of her lips and the darting artistry of her tongue, and in a matter of seconds, when he felt that he would have liked to continue for hours, cold sweat started out on his forehead and he had to break contact to gasp for air.

"Ab, are you ill again?" Her voice was threaded with concern.

He shook his head. "No ... only you slugged me a lot harder than that guy did last night. I'm not used to it."

At this point, Acy lumbered in being trailed by the doctor and Willie. Dr. Bannerman's shrewd eyes took in his patient's white but ecstatic face and did some swift mental mathematics. A glance at Cyri only revealed that her respiration was somewhat rapid, her eyes starry and her wet, unpainted lips a little more scarlet than they should ordinarily be.

"You," stated the fat, little doctor, surveying his patient, "look like hell."

Ab grinned, happily. "Looks are deceiving, Doc. If I felt any better I couldn't stand it." As he spoke, he cast a look of such utter adoration at Cyri that the Doctor stirred a little uncomfortably, as if he had peeked at a scene of extreme privacy. Mentally, he drew a line, added up his problem and made no attempt to prove the answer. He was satisfied with it as it stood.

"Your rag is screaming its head off this morning," said Acy, flourishing the paper at O'Mara. 'Handsome Young Reporter Slugged by Thug. Rescued by Unknown Marksman.' You don't suppose they got you mixed up with some other reporter, do ye? Damned if I can see any handsomeness on that Irish mug."

"I don't think I'd call him handsome, either," averred Cyri, looking at Ab critically. "Rather, I'd...."

"Yeah, I know ... cute, in an ugly sort of way like a pit bull," Ab cut in. "Thanks, all you complimentary people, but my editor's got good taste. A story breaks and here I am abed and some cub gets the credit ... no, I don't even want to read it. I'm modest."

Acy roared with laughter. "That's a good 'un ... you modest."

"Say, Doc, when do I get the x-ray?"

"Don't need any x-ray. Where'd you get that idea?"

"From me, Doctor," put in Cyri. "He fainted on his face after wandering around in the room last night or early this morning and I had to make him believe his head was caved in so he'd behave."

The doctor nodded. "All you need is a couple of days' rest, then you can go home. Your head was too hard to crack. If you have any real trouble, we'll make a picture, but I don't think you'll need one."

The next two days were the happiest Absolom O'Mara had ever spent in his entire life. Cyri was with him almost constantly and he received the full broadside of her simple forthrightness and tongue-free frankness, yet he was just as amazed at the last as he was at first. People simply weren't made up that way and yet she appeared to be standing any test he could devise to trap her.

It was late in the afternoon of the second day and Cyri was sitting on the bed, her legs drawn up, revealing a length of tan thigh that would have been the height of immodesty had any other girl done it. She simply was not aware that her leg was showing, not having that acquired sense of propriety which is automatic with so many whose subsequent actions make their propriety a shallow gesture.

"Ab, I've told you everything about me, now I want your honest opinion, do you think I'm a bad person?"

"What I think doesn't matter ..."

"Oh, but it does matter. I want you to like me, like me a lot."

"If I said that I liked you, I'd be lying," he said in a soft voice. "People can lie by telling only part of the truth, you know, but you didn't let me finish. My point is, my thinking you bad isn't what makes you so. It is only when you are convinced in your heart that you have done a wrong that it can make any impression on you."

"But I killed my father," she said, questioningly.

Ab's face was grim. "I may sound trite, honey, but as far as I'm concerned there never was a man who deserved death more. No jury in the world would convict you under those circumstances."

"What about the other things I did? I won't pretend that I didn't enjoy them. I did, more than anything in my life."

He shrugged. "I, in turn, won't pretend that it wasn't something of a shock to learn about it, but I couldn't be the one to censure you for that. Maybe I have an overblown sense of justice, but

I enjoy pleasures of the flesh too much myself to ever be caught telling someone else what to do." His face was grimly serious and white beneath the bandage. "Cyri, with your sort of honesty, wrong is awfully hard to come by. Again I say these things did not make the sort of impression upon you that is necessary for a sense of sin. To you they were moments of rare enjoyment, of unequalled delight." He shook his head. "No, Cyri. For you it was not wrong. If any wrong was done, it was done by those who were older than you and therefore more responsible."

"Then you don't dislike me because of what I've been?"

Absalom O'Mara sat bolt upright in bed and let his bright, blue eyes overflow with tears that drew snaky trails of brightness down his cheeks to drip from his chin without in the slightest attempting to pretend that they weren't there. "Don't ever ask that question again, Cyri ... not ever again."

There was a catch in her voice when she spoke. "Ab, you meant that from your very depths, didn't you?"

He nodded slowly. "I've never meant anything more in my life."

The moment was tense and both man and woman sensed electric things in the atmosphere, but before either of them could speak, Willie came in to announce that a cab was waiting below.

The light went out of Ab's eyes and the expectant tenseness from Cyri's taut muscles. He nodded at Willie.

"O.K. I'll be ready in a moment." He slid from the bed and put on his coat, having previously, put all his clothes on with the exception of his coat. He looked distractedly at Cyri who now had regained her calm air of patient waiting. "I'll be back, Cyri ... as soon as I can."

"Please do, Ab. I want you to come back." Her eyes were steady and her gaze direct.

Ab's hands clenched tightly into fists and he thrust them into his pockets, feeling like wrecking some inanimate object to ease his feelings. He had never seen the window to a heart open so wide and the interior bared so fearlessly. Again the feeling of something akin to fright tingled his diaphragm.

"Thanks a lot, Cyri ... for everything."

"I enjoyed it, Ab. I thank you for everything, too."

With a sound like a sob in his throat, he turned and followed Willie out of the room.

Daisy came and looked intently at Cyri who still sat on the bed, her eyes blank and unseeing.

"You sorta likes that man, don't you, honey?"

The girl didn't answer at once. After careful deliberation, she faced the older woman.

"How can I know, Daisy? I thought I was in love with the other one. Now I think I'm in love with this one. How will I know? How can I be sure?"

"Does you miss the other'n?"

"No, it's like he never existed at all, but when I was with him ..."

"Nemmine that. If you doesn't miss him now, then he was jes' a Saddy Night man. They's fun fer a while, but they ain't got no permanents. Wait till Mistuh O'Mara done been gone a while, then see."

"I wish Willie hadn't come in when he did," she complained without animation. "He was about to say something."

Daisy sniffed. "If that ain't jes' like a man, comin' in and breakin' up sumpn'."

"Oh, he didn't mean to, Daisy. I know he didn't."

"You quit takin' up fer that high talkin' nigger. How come he didn't stop and listen befo' he come inter the room?"

Cyri didn't answer because again she was thinking hard and staring sightlessly out of the window.

"You sure is got it bad, honey," muttered Daisy as she left the room.

Ab was at the bar thanking Acy. "Maybe I'll be able to do something for you some day, Acy, and thanks again."

"Don't deserve no … any thanks. Done it for business reasons. If you'd a conked out on me there'd go a good customer."

Ab smiled. "You're so modest and complimentary."

Acy grinned in return. "And you're so cute … like a pit bulldog."

Ab flushed a little. "I'll get you for that," he promised as he went through the door.

O'Mara visited police headquarters before going home and talked to Lt. Eccles.

"What did you do with Lamb, Maurice?"

Eccles scratched a match on the sole of his shoe and tried to light a soggy cigar. "Couldn't do a thing. We'll make the assault with a dangerous weapon stick on Mack Pitre and he'll go to Angola, but Lamb insists that he just happened to be parked there and ran when the shooting started. Pitre supports him in it, says he was alone, and won't talk except to say he didn't like you and clipped you for that reason. We know the truth, but we can't prove it."

"So," growled Ab, "I've got to stay in after dark for the rest of my life … is that it?"

"Why?" asked Eccles.

"Because, you dumb flattie, the minute he gets a chance, he'll tee off on me again … one of his thugs will anyhow. I might not be so lucky next time."

Eccles grinned. "Why don't you advertise for the guy that pulled you out of it this time. He'd be handy to have as a body guard. He's a cinch shot with that twenty two and he never kills anyone. Lamb only has a sore head, like you, and Pitre is as full of holes as a sieve, but he'll live. He used hollow point bullets that deliver a hell of a wallop, but they didn't penetrate very deep. Mack only has one dangerous wound and he was hit six times."

Ab whistled softly. "What did the guy have, a machine gun?"

"Sure looked that way. He missed once, the one that went through the back glass and the windshield of Lamb's car. Missed him by half an inch, but the error was corrected on the next shot. Actually, I believe he could have killed either of them with no trouble. One of those bullets through the head would have made egg custard out of their brains."

"B-rr," shuddered Ab. "Lay off, will you. I'm still queasy about the belly."

"Tell you what, Ab," said Eccles. "I can give you a permit to carry a gun and if those mugs lay into you again, blast 'em. You'll be doing the city a service. So far, Lamb has kept his nose clean … apparently, but you know it isn't so. There isn't a dirty foul racket in town that he isn't either running or has a finger in, at least. We know it, as I say, but we can't prove it. With him on a slab, we wouldn't need to prove anything."

O'Mara seemed attracted by the idea. "Might not be a bad thought at that. I used to be a pretty good shot while I was in service. I'll bet I killed more sharks with a .45 than Boynton did Japs."

"O.K., I'll fix it up." Eccles opened a drawer to his desk. "You like .45's?"

"Yeah … that's all I ever shot. I can field strip 'em blindfolded."

"Here, take this one. We took it off a mug the other day. It's in good shape."

"Jesus, what a nickel job." Ab took the bright weapon and hefted it lovingly. "That shoulder holster go with it?"

"Well," Eccles was reluctant. "That's a mighty good holster. I sort of had my eye on it myself."

"I'll give it back after I've chilled Lamb." He slipped off his coat and donned the holster and placed the heavy automatic in it. "It'll make me walk with a list, but brother, there ain't nothing in the world that gives quite the confidence that hunk of metal does. Thanks, Eccles. Oh, got my extra ammo? I'll want to practice some."

Eccles handed him a carton of ammunition. "This belonged to the owner of the pistol. He won't miss it."

"Where is he?"

"Six feet under, I'd say. He scattered his brains all over a room with that gun."

Ab grimaced. "Now I won't be able to eat dinner."

The next three days were unalloyed torture for Ab. He had a murder to cover in which a lady of questionable antecedents, but unquestionable aim, had pointed a gun in the general direction of her bohemian comrade and pulled the trigger seven times. Every shot went home, making said comrade a very repellent object indeed, since the bullets had come from a weapon of heavy caliber and were liberally scattered from navel to forehead. This took long tedious hours of his time; then a passenger plane had mistaken a stretch of swamp water for an unlighted runway in a thin drizzle and had spread itself and certain vital parts of thirty passengers over a wide area of swamp, necessitating a trip into same, towing a partly drunken photographer who complained bitterly about the mud, the rain, the mosquitoes that descended upon them in swarms, and something that was a woeful oversight on the part or parts of certain power or powers who had failed to provide this endless jungle with the proper facilities for slaking the thirst. This took time, energy and the remnants of an already badly rent state of religion that Absalom could ill afford to rend further.

Cyri, for the first time in her life, was distraught and nervous. She tried to wear herself out at tennis, but this only earned her muttered diatribes from the females, whom she trounced with even more soundness than usual. She tried to read and found that she couldn't. She tried to get Acy to let her help Willie 'tend bar, but this Acy would not have and no amount of threat or cajolery could move him.

Ab had been gone for nearly three days when at noon of the third day, he called her. She fought her leaping heart to calmness and answered. He was sorry, he said, that he had been too busy to call or see her. He had been busy, he was sorry because as he had been busy he hadn't had … He stopped because her melodic laughter came to him over the wire.

"What's so funny," he demanded.

"You are," she replied.

"Well, I asked for it and I got it. What are you doing this afternoon?"

"Nothing."

"What say we ride out on the lake and practice with a new pistol I have, with which I have intentions of blasting one Lamb should he make any further efforts to split my skull?"

"Oh, Ab, do you think he might try to get you again?"

"One never knows, honey. I'll pick you up about one. I'm wearing shorts, so dress comfortably."

She did and chose a pair of white shorts and a deep green T shirt, making Ab quiver weakly in the region of his solar plexus. He had borrowed an automobile from a fellow reporter who had borrowed sufficient money from Ab for a payment on the vehicle and Ab insisted on being repaid in mileage.

They chose an isolated spot on the beach, far enough from human habitation to be safe in using the weapon and Ab set up a tin can fifteen paces away and hit it three times out of seven. He turned proudly to Cyri who was sitting on the remains of an old cypress log watching him and said, "Nothing to it, chicken. You point, squeeze off, and sometimes you hit. Want to try it?"

Her face was solemn. "It seems a little morbid out here practicing to kill someone whom you fear may try to kill you. It's depressing."

"Oh, quite," he agreed lightly. "Only I don't think he'll try again. This lovely pistol is just insurance. Come here and let me teach you."

She moved to her feet with a single sinuous move and stood beside him.

"Now," he said in his best instructor's voice, "you hold it like so, thusly. Not too tight, not too loose … No, don't grip with the thumb. Let it rest easily at the side without gripping with it. Now, see this gismo here at the muzzle? That's the sight. You hold it right at the bottom of the target, the can in this case, then you notch it in this little fersteris on the back of the slide. Then, holding steady, you press the trigger, squeeze it gently, don't jerk it. Now try it once."

She did, standing as he told her, arm out from the shoulder, other hand on her hip, relaxed but not limp.

Ab was so intent on her natural, easy grace and the delightfully sculptured length of her tawny legs that he was somewhat startled when the explosion came. Her eyes lighted and she showed the nearest thing to excitement he had ever seen her exhibit.

"I hit it, Ab. I hit it."

"Yeah," he said, amazed. "You sure did. Here, let me get you another can. That one has too many holes in it. He procured another, but smaller can, and set it on the stump for her.

"Hey, hold that thing in another direction. That's one of the cardinal rules of the hunt. Never point the gun at anyone."

Her smile was roguish. "I'm sorry ... but how will you hit Lamb if you don't point the gun at him?"

"Shaddup ... go on now, and let me see you hit that. I made a bull the first time I shot one too."

"That was easy," she scoffed. "Watch ..." Again the pistol exploded, the empty cartridge case spun in a frenetic little gold spangled parabola and again the can clanked dismally and disappeared. This time Ab had to retrieve it from a tangle of sword grass.

"This ceases to be a joke," he said with a frown as he replaced the can. "You can't do it again."

The third bullet gutted the can in such a manner that a fresh one had to be found. The fourth shot missed and Ab chuckled. "I knew it couldn't last."

"You're in worse luck now than ever," she told him. "I found out something I've been doing wrong. It won't happen again."

"What?"

"Never mind. Put the can back."

In rapid succession, the fifth, sixth, and seventh shots went home and Ab sat suddenly in the sand and moaned. "I'll never be able to face my fellow man again. You, to whom a pistol is something cowboys shoot blanks with in movies, take an old hand down like it was nothing. It ain't human."

She kicked some sand on him and a race ensued, which, in his weakened condition, O'Mara lost in the first fifty yards.

"Come back and fight like a man," he bellowed. "You not only out shoot me, but you out run me. What you're doing to me shouldn't happen to a dog."

She trotted back to him and he noted that her respiration was only slightly increased. Again came that inundating tide of emotion that shook him with such violence that it left his face pale.

"What's the matter, Ab … Oh, you shouldn't have run like that so soon after your injury." She came close, her eyes soft with concern.

He waved his hand. "Sit down, Cyri."

She obeyed and noticed the smooth play of his muscles beneath his pink-white skin.

"Did you," he began, "ever have something to sweep over you suddenly and make you want to cry, make you weak and shuddery inside, make you feel like the sudden onset of some vague illness."

"Yes, I think so."

"You do that to me sometimes, Cyri, and when you do, I want you in my arms so badly that it hurts like … like my head did that night."

"Then why don't you?"

"I was hoping you'd say something like that," he whispered hoarsely. His arms were strong about her and the smooth skin of his back was cool to her touch, but his lips were hot, hungry, and searching. A tremor of resistance went through her muscles as his knee probed gently at hers, to relax almost instantly as the pressure grew stronger. Her arms grew tighter about the neck as the leg progressed and the first leaping throb of her own swiftly rising passion whipped through her. Again a wild, uncontrollable weakness took O'Mara's breath and reduced him to gasping.

"Cyri … Let's get away from here … I … you …" He shook his head and rose unsteadily to his feet.

She leaped up and came again into his arms, holding his face firmly in her hands. "Ab, what's the matter. I've got to know."

He laughed shakily. "Just now I did something no gentleman does, on his first date anyway. When you kiss me I just turn to water and leak away. I can't stand it. I …" Her lips covered his again and the silken touch of the fine skin of her thighs against his own almost made him cry out.

When she released him this time, he caught her purposefully by the arm. "Home you go, honey. I wouldn't trust myself with you out here, and you're going to be no help at all. I can see that."

"Why," she asked, "do you need help?"

"Because if I don't get it …" He stopped, appalled by what he was about to say.

"Are you afraid?"

"Yes," he almost shouted. "I'm afraid."

"I'm not and I want you to."

He stopped and stared at her. "Honey, will you make me a promise. Let me get used to you by degrees, will you?"

She shrugged. "I'll make the promise if you wish. I won't swear I'll keep it."

"Get in that automobile before I spank the lovely, textured surface upon which you sit."

They rode slowly back toward Canal Street in silence, till Ab said despairingly. "Honey, you're much wiser than me. What's going to happen to us?"

"I won't put it in words, Ab, but I know. I know also that you'll make yourself unhappy if you don't quit begging trouble. Why can't you enjoy me like I enjoy you?"

"Because I'm a product of civilization and somehow it never reached you. You're still as fundamental as Eve and I'll be damned if I know how you managed it."

"Where do you live, Ab?"

"Over on St. Charles Avenue. Strictly the ritz. There's three of us who stay there. One is an engineer on the Inland Waterway, barges, tugs, and stuff. The other is a med student. Works like a Trojan ... never home hardly and then he's half dead. Why?"

"Nothing, I just thought I'd like to see it."

Ab beamed brightly. "Sure, I'll show it to you right now. It's really a nice place."

He assisted her from the car in front of a big, brick apartment building. He buzzed, then shook his head. "Figured I'd have to use my key ... but the thing's open. Isn't closed till night. I must be thinking about something else." He opened the door and allowed her to precede him into the building.

CHAPTER TEN
—LESTER BIDS GOODBYE

THEY TRAVERSED a long hall and Ab unlocked a door. Cyri stood in the middle of the small but neat living room and turned slowly around on her heels making the long, flat muscles show in her legs. Ab shook himself doggedly and went into the bedroom to put the pistol up. Cyri bounced on the couch to test its springiness, then went into the little kitchen. It was clean and compact with everything in place.

"Someone is a good housekeeper," she called out. "Couldn't be you, could it?"

"I'm the best you ever saw," he said, coming into the kitchen. "How do you like it?"

"Wonderful … and three men stay here? I'd never believe it. I notice even the beds are made."

"My touch again," he said lightly. "Cyri, would you excuse me a moment while I wash some of the sand off me? I'm as gritty as a wet rock."

"Go ahead. I'll wander around and poke into things."

She sat in a deep, comfortable chair and clenched her hands against the leaping fire that seemed determined to consume her. Her thighs still ached from the touch of his insistent knee. She clenched them fiercely for a moment and breathed deeply, striving to quell the tumult in her breast. She recalled the feeling that she had for Rod, and so pale was it that she was moved to chuckle at her own lack of sophistication. Rod had never opened the veil for her to peer behind. Ab did not do it willingly at first, but it didn't matter. She saw him as he was with or without his wish. He would open up in time she felt sure. She seemed to sense that Ab was a man who would welcome someone to whom he might bare himself.

With sudden resolution tightening her jaw, she kicked off her shoes and tiptoed into the bedroom. She could see the bath because he hadn't bothered to close the door, thinking that she would stay in the living room. He was fiddling with the shower that occupied half of the rather large bath, trying to get the right temperature of water. With a swift movement, she moved closer to him and stood for a moment like a slim tan shaft of the purest ivory. Then with a leap, she was in the bathroom. Another step and the sting of cold water struck her skin, immediately paled by the greater shock of his water slick body as she rushed into his arms, forcing him under the water.

"Oh, my God, Cyri …" His cry was heavy with stupefaction and something deeper and more fundamental, than his arms were crushing steel bands about her and the water sent jagged, trickling knives searching for tiny spaces in their close, crushed bodies.

The sobbing cries that welled into her throat became only throaty gurgles of sound, so savage was the assault of his lips. Her own were hurt and bruised, but she reveled in the pain and gave all the pressure of her own muscular, young body.

Suddenly Ab's grip slackened and his mouth withdrew from hers. "No … No… Cyri … … we can't …we can't. I love you, can't you see that? I love you, Cyri." A motion of her lubricous body made him cry out. "Cyri, I can't stand it."

"You don't love me," she cried accusingly. "If you did, you wouldn't do me this way. Please, Ab …"

She felt herself swept from her feet by a miraculous return of his strength, then the rough nap of the counterpane touched her back. Things lost their shape and became monstrous and unreal. The touch of him affected her skin like a beneficent fire that scorched and yet soothed her, but his dalliance was driving her mad.

She was a delightfully rare confectionary that he seemed intent on tasting in all her various ingredients, painting a trail of unendurable desire over her body. She proffered twin hillocks of agonizing delight that slowly transferred its dull thunders to the skin of her thighs. Begging entreaty; and suddenly she caught her breath just as his lips came squarely down upon hers. There was exquisite, choking ecstasy that flooded upward and suffused her body, blurring her sight further and setting in motion something that had no actual beginning, only a becoming. Like a mighty arpeggio, it twittered through her blood, sending it gushing in turgid flooding thrusts, hammering against the tocsin of her brain, working up a crescendo that threw her from manic exultation to boneless relaxation. In the distance there seemed to be the deep thrumming of a single stringed bass viol across which an endless bow was being drawn. She rested in a lifeless, shuddering heap with pink and blue clouds forming a support of indescribable softness floating, floating nowhere and for nothing.

Ab buried his face in her masses of fragrant hair and strove to quell the harsh sobs that rose in his throat. At that moment, he was certain that his senses had taken leave for all times. His brain was a madly whirling vortex in which fragments of thought, tattered beyond all recognition, floated like debris in a flood. A tautness had snapped within him, and from it poured all the poisonous accumulation of his soul, gathered and grimly stored since his childhood.

The ringing of the doorbell snapped them back to reality with painful suddenness. Ab let go a string of blistering oaths, and then said to Cyri, "Stay right where you are and I'll shut the door. Whoever it is will be sent packing."

Cyri let herself sink back into her powdery reveries, a smile of utter contentment touching her lush lips, her eyes drowsy and pearly. She could hear voices in the living room, but in her present state, they didn't register and yet one of them was definitely unpleasant. It pricked through the rosy haze and initiated a faint irritated resentment within her. Then, through the mist, came two words that yanked her from her drowse like the searing stab of a naked electric wire.

Growling oaths to himself, Ab opened the door and found himself pushed back into the room by a soft, fragrant hand.

"Sit down, Mr. O'Mara," said the soft, reptilian voice of Lester Lamb. The unwavering muzzle of the pistol he held lent a certain authority to the demand, so Ab complied with the icy certainty that here, at long last, was *it*. Cyri couldn't help and if she saw what happened, she'd certainly wind up on a slab beside him. Keep out, Cyri, keep out, Cyri, keep out, Cyri. Over and over his agonized brain beamed the appeal to her. Keep out, for God's sake, *keep out*.

"Mr. O'Mara, I'm going to kill you," said the sibilant voice.

Ab nodded without consciously hearing the threat. His every mental reaction was a silent warning to Cyri to stay out of the living room.

"You presumed to interfere where it did not concern you and I am not the sort of man who cares for that sort of thing. I was a fool to leave the matter to an underling. I admit it. Mistake is the lot of humanity due to certain imperfections which it is too late to correct. Genius, however, comes in the ability to correct mistakes. I am, this afternoon, correcting one of mine which I did not at the time anticipate. Regrettable, I'm sure, but necessary ..." He stopped and his glance moved and stopped, frozen to the bedroom door.

Ab wheeled about and there in the doorway stood Cyri holding the brightly nickled .45 in her hand, steady and leveled. With slow, fearless grace, she moved forward like the beginning of a dance.

"You're not going to kill anyone." Her voice was flatly metallic. She continued to move toward Lamb who took three steps backward and leaned against the door.

"Stop," he said, his voice strained and cracking. "I have a gun trained on your heart."

Still she moved toward him, her eyes boiling hells of green flame. "I have a gun trained on yours. Let's see who'll pull the trigger first."

"Stop her, O'Mara," screamed Lamb, his face rutted and white, bathed with sweat.

Ab opened his mouth but only a hoarse croak came out. His limbs were numb with a heavy paralysis that held him helpless in his chair.

"Stop her, O'Mara," shrieked Lamb, again his own gun trembling in a ragged circle. Still he did not seem able to pull the trigger. There was something terrifying in her slow, inexorable advance.

"I'll shoot," he screamed, pushing back against the door in a frenzy of numb terror. "I'll shoot ... so help me, I'll ..."

There was a cataclysmic explosion and another and another. Ab's eyes went momentarily dull and unseeing, his ears stunned by the shattering explosions of the gun in the confined area of the room. His eyes focused again to see the body of Lamb nailed, it seemed, to the door, his hands tearing with slow, terrible strength at his shirt in an effort to stem the awful agony.

His gun spilled over a clutching wrist and fell to the floor, and a fourth explosion rocked the room, and this time the clutching hands fluttered downward, lax and limp. Lamb then crumpled forward and fell with that curious bouncing impact that spells death.

Ab suddenly regained his senses and leaped to his feet. "Darling, are you all right, are you all right, are you … are you …?"

"Oh, quit fluttering and jabbering, Ab," she said calmly holding out the gun butt foremost. "I let the hammer down. It's perfectly safe now."

He took her in his arms like a dying man holding onto life. He stood away after a moment and swallowed a lump in his throat the size of a pineapple. "Go into the other room, darling. There'll be police here in a moment."

She smiled and went back into the bedroom while Ab sat soddenly in his chair and dialed a number on the phone. The line was busy. Again he lived the sight of her walking with mechanical objectivity across the floor, without a single article of clothing on her outrageously lovely body, the gun held with rigid purpose … He twitched. The sight must have been too much for Lamb because from the time she came through the door, he hadn't a chance. Not once had the palsied gun he held been even a threat. He dialed again and this time he got through to Eccles.

"Maurice?"

"Yeah."

"You can come get him."

"Come get who?"

"Lamb."

"The hell you say … where?"

"In my apartment … and Maurice, there'll be something a little queer here and if you want me to be here when you arrive, you'll pick a group of men you can trust to keep their mouths shut. Is it a deal?"

"Sure, but ..."

"No buts, fella. A promise or you'll have to wait for your story."

"O.K., I'll be there in ten minutes."

A hammering on the door made Ab run into the bedroom. "You stay right here, chicken. I don't want anyone to see you ... gimme that gun, in case that's any of Lamb's mob."

He opened the door and shoved the gun into the midsection of a stringy old maid who promptly screamed and fainted. There were half a dozen other tenants grouped about the door, but there were several more screams and a general flight when Ab presented the gun.

"It's O.K. folks. There's been some trouble but the police are on the way here now."

The body had been disposed of and Eccles' men had left. "Now where's the girl. I want to talk to her."

"But there's no reason to talk to her. I tell you I did it ..."

"I know you told me that and you've told me ten times. So many times that I smell something. Now ... oh, hello, Cyri. You can come on out, the men have gone."

She came out arrayed in her shorts and T shirt, smiling and utterly at ease, though the sight of her marvelously smooth, long, young limbs was visibly disturbing to the men.

"Tell me your side of the story, Cyri," requested Eccles, gently.

"Don't say anything," begged Ab, dashing a sudden precipitation of sweat from his forehead.

"Why not?" she wanted to know. "I don't know why you've been telling him you did it."

Ab groaned and flopped unhappily in a chair. "I give up," he said, throwing up his hands.

"Good," enthused Eccles. "Now maybe I can get the straight of this thing." He nodded encouragingly at the girl, a little shaken by her flawless composure. By rights she should be screaming with hysterics and flopping about yelling for ammonia, a doctor, a hospital, and saying she was being persecuted by the police.

"Well, Ab was afraid it might be someone … like Lamb, so I stayed in the room."

"Why didn't you take the gun with you if you thought it was him," was Eccles merciless question.

"Well, er … You see, I wasn't sure."

"If Cyri wasn't here I'd tell you where you give me a pain," snorted the Lieutenant scathingly. "Go on, Cyri, what happened then?"

"I don't know what made me hear those two words, but I did. They sort of struck through … you see, I was in a kind of fog and wasn't paying any attention." Ab drew up into a hard knot. If she wasn't careful, she'd tell him everything.

"I heard the words 'kill you' and I got up and grabbed the gun. It was on the dresser."

"Where were you," asked Eccles and Ab shut his eyes tightly, feeling a trickle of sweat course down his spine.

"I was on the bed," she said frankly. "So I got up and grabbed the gun and walked out into the living room and shot him as he held a gun on Ab."

"How many times did you shoot him?"

"Four."

Eccles looked at Ab who appeared on the verge of fainting. "There you are. You said three times and you were a liar on the face of it. The man had four bullet holes in him … in a spot I could cover with my hand. Where did you learn to shoot, Cyri?"

"Out at the lake," she said simply. "Ab taught me how this afternoon."

Eccles pinched his face between his hands, having the odd sensation that he was squeezing someone else's face.

"I believe you because I have to," he said to the girl.

"You don't have to," she told him sweetly, without rancor, "but you should."

"Why?" he asked, a little annoyed and inclined toward bluntness himself.

Her smile was seraphic. "Because it's the truth."

"Hah," exploded O'Mara triumphantly. "If that doesn't hold you, just talk to her long enough and something will. I promise it."

Eccles sighed. "I think I'm learning what you mean. Tell me, Cyri, how can you sit there as calm as ditch water after having killed a man?"

"Now blast you, Maurice, that was a low blow. Cut it out and I mean now." Ab was on his feet, his fists doubled, his eyes shooting blue sparks.

"Sit down, Ab," said Cyri, quietly. Ab sat and was furious with himself for doing so.

"I'll tell the Lieutenant anything he wants to know."

"I'm sorry," said Eccles, slowly. "You don't have to answer that. It was out of line and I apologize. I'd still like to know, however."

"He was standing there with a gun in his hand. He had said he would kill Ab. He had tried once. What else was there for me to do but kill him? What should I be doing, weeping or something?"

Eccles mentally clutched himself to keep from falling into space. "Er ... no, I guess not, although ... No, I will not enumerate the things I can think of that other women would have done under like circumstances."

"Somehow," mused the girl, thoughtfully, "I don't seem to be like other women." Her living form was more than ample proof of that.

Eccles looked fixedly at the ceiling and whistled a thin tune off key and Ab groaned. Eccles looked back at her for a moment, then said, "You know, I wouldn't be at all surprised if you're right, my dear."

Ab gritted his teeth noisily. "You ... *you* ... you don't know anything. You should have been sitting crucified to this chair like I was and watched her walking across the floor in slow motion, with that bastard screaming at her every step that he'd shoot if she didn't stop and she never did stop. She shot him while she was still walking toward him."

"Holy cow, Cyri," burst out Eccles, "why in God's name did you do that?"

She shrugged. "Well, I was afraid I'd miss him if I didn't get pretty close. You see, I just learned to shoot this afternoon."

"You should have been here," muttered Ab, automatically.

"I don't think I'd have liked that," said Cyri with a vixenish grin.

Ab looked up in surprise. Eccles asked, "Why not?"

The grin widened. "Because I wasn't quite ready for visitors."

Eccles jingled silver in his pocket and stared numbly at a repulsive chromo on the wall that had once adorned a calendar.

Absalom O'Mara shaved a faint so closely that he had to clutch the arm of the chair, then blood rushed to his face so madly that he knew it would pop out.

"We ...," croaked Ab, frantically. "We ... we ... we."

Eccles went into an earthquake of laughter. "We ... we ... we ..." he gasped. "What the devil ..." Another roar of mirth burst from him and Ab turned the color of port wine.

"What I'm trying to say, you ass, is that we're married." He looked miserably at Cyri and not liking what he saw, amended the statement. "That is, we will be in a little while … won't we, darling?" His plea was plaintive and thick with a love that was greater than himself.

She bounced up and sat on his lap. "Ab, do you mean that … please don't play with me."

"Certainly I mean it," he choked. "Now … right now. Immediately … right now."

Eccles wiped his eyes, mirth still tugging at his diaphragm. *"Tout a l'heure* is a good word for right now," he said. "French, I think you've used up all the English synonyms."

"Go to blazes," growled Ab. "We'll need you as a witness."

"In that case," grinned Eccles, "you'll have to go there, too. Christ, if you could have seen your face." He exploded into laughter again.

"Lieutenant," said Cyri with hopeful seriousness, "I hope you won't think any less of Ab and me because I said something I shouldn't. I love him and he loves me. Isn't that enough reason?"

Eccles sobered instantly. "Why, kid … hell's bells." He leaned over and kissed her on the cheek. "Who am I to tell people what to do as long as they don't break the law. I just happen to have found out that there is a lot I don't know about people. Whatever you and Ab did is your own business and it was *right*. Anyway," he said, grinning, "the sapsucker might never have proposed if you hadn't let me in on it."

CHAPTER ELEVEN
—AN ORPHAN TAKES HER MAN

THERE WAS a party of noble proportions in progress in Acy's quarters. In a heavily upholstered chair on one side of a thick-legged cherry wood table sat Father Alberti Francioni, short, red and round of face with a tiny horseshoe circlet of hair as thin as a mustache about the back of his head. The dome was glistening smooth and steaming somewhat as he had taken aboard a fairly modest cargo of fifteen year old rye that Acy had dug up. Acy sat across from him with a bowl of boiled eggs and rye wafers and Willie had disinterred the monster beer schooner for the occasion. It now brimmed with bock and Acy's upper lip was white from the collar. He wiped it off with a thumb and forefinger. Eccles sat near Acy, his eyes staring in fascination at the dusty bottle from which had come such elegant nectar. On a third side of the table sat Absalom O'Mara and Cyri Malnoir O'Mara, vintage of the same day.

"How," Acy wanted to know, "did you find out she was living with me?"

The little priest's eyes twinkled brightly. "First I learned through the sheriff, who learned from 'A friend of justice.' This friend wrote an anonymous letter giving the information which he probably thought would stir up trouble. He did not know that immediately after I learned of Cyri's, er, escape, I made an investigation into the matter, using the Grand Jury as a front.

Old Alphonse Quebedeaux was a great help … you remember him, Cyri?"

"Yes, sir. He gave me five dollars when I left." Her eyes were misty soft.

"Well, Mr. Jones, the Grand Jury unearthed a long career of shiftlessness, neglect, and brutality. Judging from other acts, it was agreed that it was within the realm of possibility that he had acted as Cyri said. They returned a no true bill. When all this about Lamb came out in the newspaper, I felt it my duty to come down here and let her know what had been done."

Ab grinned. "And got here in time to tie a knot. I think Cyri would have rather had you do it than anyone in the world." The girl did not speak, but her eyes were eloquent. Ab rose to his feet. "And now, good people, we will leave you and take a ten block honeymoon."

Father Francioni nodded understandingly, but Acy snorted. "That don't sound like no honeymoon to me. Why the eclipse?"

Ab pointed to Cyri. "Ask her. It's her idea."

Cyri said. "What makes people think that a train or automobile trip will make for more enjoyment of the first few weeks of marriage? I think that if a trip is to be made, it should come at least a month later. I believe that any couple who start out in familiar surroundings without a lot of fanfare will do a lot better."

Eccles cleared his throat. "As I was told several days ago, under similar circumstances, 'If that don't hold you, just keep talking and something else will.' You should know better. I had an excuse!"

"Nuunfff," sniffed Acy, pinking a little. "Git, er, get on about your rag picking. We got partyin' to do."

The girl bent over him and kissed him full upon the mouth. "I'm not going to try to thank you, Acy," she said, "for everything you've done. I'm just going to love you with all my heart … always."

"A fair trade," he muttered huskily as he squeezed her close for a moment. "Come back and visit, Sugar, any chance you get."

"I'll come often, Acy, I really will." She turned to Willie who stood in the doorway, looking funereal, with Daisy just behind him, weeping silently. "Willie, Daisy … both of you, I do appreciate everything you did for me. I'll never forget it."

Daisy dashed out and folded the girl in her arms for a moment, then fled weeping loudly.

Willie swallowed audibly. "You'll always be our Princess," he said, his voice quivering from emotion. "We would welcome the opportunity to do it all over again."

A sob caught in her throat and she turned away, followed by her husband.

For several minutes after they left, there was dead, stagnant silence in the living room. Eccles broke the silence by tinkling the ice in his glass and Father Francioni cleared his throat.

"Maybe you can explain that girl to me, Father," suggested Eccles. "I saw her thirty minutes after she had shot Lamb and it apparently had had no more effect on her than breaking a fingernail. Since then, I have come to expect such an attitude from her, but I still don't get it."

Acy gruffed deeply. "Me neither. She's been here better'n two years and she can still pop my eyeballs with some of the things she comes out with."

The little priest poured a drink and holding it up to the light, gazed intently through its rich amber clarity. "I doubt that I could prove a single thing I'm about to say, but I will, nevertheless, say it. None of us can deny with any authority that although God made nature self-energizing, he doesn't enjoy occasional experimentation. I could probably be defrocked for heresy, should this get about, but I can even detect a touch of rare humor in some of these experiments.

"The girl has never needed the myriad of compensations to which we mortals cling so frantically. Consequently, she has no need for spiritual protection. This sort of thing can be demoralizing to someone who is not similarly constructed. She uses none of the conventional evasions inherent in man, not because she doesn't care for them, but because she doesn't need them. Anything less than a spade to her is frankly a lie … dishonesty. God placed that child in a veritable quagmire of adverse environment from which she emerged experienced, but absolutely undefiled, and I say this as a man, not a priest. As a man of the cloth, there are other considerations which would make my evaluation shape up differently."

"If I may say so, sir," said Willie with astonishment, "that, coming from a clergyman, is little short of cataclysmic, antithetical."

Father Francioni smiled grimly. "Yes, I suppose it is, but is there any reason why a priest should necessarily be a fool?"

Willie's bowed head acknowledged the rebuke.

"She came to the sheriff," he continued, "and told him in plain straight language just what she had done. In equally plain language, she told him why she had done it. Then she shut up and only answered questions."

Acy mopped a perspiring brow. "I know how that is. She told me the story in about twenty words."

"She seems," mused Father Francioni, "to have a shockingly mathematical mind and once it is made up, her inner self is reassured … therefore, she is not given to an act, then a sudden awakening, and consequent remorse. Remorse is merely the tribute which conscience pays to stupidity."

Eccles whipped out a notebook. "Mind if I take that down?"

"Do so, by all means," the little man said, smiling. "However, I may have bent an already famous remark to suit my purpose."

"I'll take the bent version," said Eccles, writing rapidly.

"Now I don't know this, Lieutenant, but I should say that Cyri could have given an excellent reason for killing Lamb, maybe several."

"She gave several," Eccles nodded quickly. "All of them unanswerable."

"So I thought," said the priest. "As I said, she had justified the act in her own mind before committing it, therefore, she saw no cause for rending her clothes and indulging in a lot of capers with which I am extremely short tempered anyway, and inclined to suspect as being produced for outside consumption on one hand and personal expiation on the other."

Acy handed Willie the schooner, suggestively, with one hand and reached for an egg with the other. "Fill 'er, Willie. I want to offer a toast ... fill up, gentlemen." Drinks were poured and Acy stood and raised his newly filled schooner. "Gentlemen, I give you women in general."

Eccles made a move with his drink, then came to an abrupt halt. "What for?" he asked almost rudely.

Acy grinned. "Because then I wish to give you Mrs. Cyri O'Mara and Absalom O'Mara and I thought the contrast would be such as to cause a chuckle and possibly some satisfaction."